Darktown
Strutters

Darktown Strutters

A Novel

Wesley Brown

Afterword by W. T. Lhamon Jr.

UNIVERSITY OF MASSACHUSETTS PRESS AMHERST

Library of Congress Cataloging-in-Publication Data

Brown, Wesley, 1945–
Darktown strutters: a novel / Wesley Brown ; afterword by W.T. Lhamon Jr.
        p.   cm.
Includes bibliographical references.
ISBN 1-55849-270-4 (pbk. : alk. paper)
1. Rice, Tom, 1808–1860—Fiction. 2. Afro-Americans in the
performing arts—Fiction. 3. Blackface entertainers—Fiction.
4. Minstrel shows—Fiction. 5. Race relations—Fiction.
I. Title.

PS3552.R7382 D37 2000
813'.54—dc21   00-055177

British Library Cataloguing in Publication data are available.

For my grandmother, Annie Davidson Brown (1886–1935), whom I met in my father's stories and missed whenever he told me anything about her.

America is the land of masking jokers. We wear the mask for purposes of aggression as well as for defense when we are projecting the future and preserving the past. In short, the motives behind the mask are as numerous as the ambiguities the mask conceals.

RALPH ELLISON

If you're going to tell people the truth, you'd better make them laugh.

GEORGE BERNARD SHAW

CONTENTS

Darktown
Strutters

A traveling show was passing through Kentucky in 1830. One day while the show was playing in Louisville, an actor named Thomas Rice was walking around the back of the theater. He heard a stomping sound coming from inside a livery stable and decided to find out what it was. Rice stepped inside and picked up a foul smell coming from loaves of horse manure. Feed was scattered everywhere and horses were snorting in stalls. Then he saw a black man whose whole body looked like it was having a fit of the hiccups. There seemed to be something lopsided about him. His right side from the chest into the shoulder, down past the ribs through the hips and legs, was bulging with muscles. But his left shoulder and leg were drawn up and stiff looking. At first Rice thought the man was crippled. Then he realized he wasn't limping at all; he was dancing. When he saw Rice watching him, he stopped. He didn't say anything but waited to see what this white man would do, whose legs were a fancy bootful up to the knees. Rice straightened up, ran his hand along the lapel of his waistcoat, and took a few steps forward.

"Don't stop on my account," Rice said.

"Beg pardon, sir?"

"What was that you were doing?"

"They call it rockin the heel."

"You rock a damn good heel!"

"Thank you. I take a bit a pleasure in it myself."

"What they call you?"

"Name's Jim Crow, sir."

1

"Well, Jim Crow, you think you might be able to show a game-legged fella like myself how to rock the heel?"

"I'll give it a try."

Before Rice could blink, Crow dangled his body like he was strung together with thread. And in a voice on the harsh side of rust, he said the same words over and over again.

Wheel about/turn about/do just so
and every time I wheel about/I jump Jim Crow!

Every time he said this, he jumped straight up; and when he landed, he'd rock the heel of his left foot. Rice couldn't believe the way Crow turned his knees in and then toe-stomped his foot into the ground.

Rice made it his business to stop by and see Crow at the stable every day. One night after a show, he ran out of the theater in a fever. When Rice got to a section of ramshackle cabins, he realized he had no idea where Jim Crow lived. A woman chewing on a stick and carrying a bucket breathing steam stopped to stare at him.

"That you Kentucky?" she said.

"Excuse me," Rice said, moving closer. "You know where Jim Crow lives?"

"Fix me Lord, 'fore I start mistakin slavery for free!"

"What's that?"

"Just saying to myself how much you favor Kentucky, a buggy driver for the Churchills. But it was just Mister Tricks playin with me."

"Mister Tricks?"

"Just another name for evenin."

"Oh....Is there a Jim Crow around here?"

"Right there," she said, using the stick in her mouth to point.

"Thank you."

"Excuse me, mister, but I think your color is quittin on you."

"What?" Rice touched his face. He'd forgotten to wipe the cork off. "Oh! I forgot all about this," he said.

"Kentucky forgets too," she said, laughing.

Rice started to ask what she meant but decided to let this woman with her strange way of talking go on about her business. Before knocking on the door, he took a handkerchief out of his pocket and wiped off as much of the burnt cork as he could.

A woman with roped charcoal gray hair stood in the doorway.

"Excuse me. I was told Jim Crow lives here."

"Jim," she said, stepping aside to let Rice in.

There was something about the way his name came out of her mouth that said everything she felt about him. Jim was sitting in a rocker, and a young boy stood a few feet away. The boy stared at Rice like he was trying to figure out what he was looking at.

"Jim! You won't believe what happened at the show tonight!"

"You can never tell. I just might."

"I used that dance you showed me and the audience called me back to do it again three times!"

"I got no trouble believin that at all."

"What would you say if I told you I'm gonna make it a regular part of the show?"

"There ain't much I can say about something you gonna do, Mister Rice."

"But you showed me how to do it!"

"That ain't what I did. What I did was show you how I do it. I couldn't give you that dance even if I wanted to. Now if you do somethin with what I showed you, that makes it yours. Then you ain't gotta ask nobody if you can use it. It belongs to you. And that's different from just copyin somebody."

"So you think I'm copyin you?"

"Mister Rice, you white. You don't need me to tell you what you doin."

"You know, I could make trouble for you. Talkin to me that way."

"Like I said, Mister Rice. You white."

"You remember that Tom Rice that came through here with that travelin show about a year back?" Whisper asked Jim.

"What about him?"

"He turned out to be another kind a white man."

"What kind is that?"

"Well, there's the kind like Crow that name you. And then there's the kind like Rice that claim you. I heard today he been travelin all over the country doin the dance you showed him and callin himself Tom 'Jim Crow' Rice."

"So?"

"It just looks like to me that our real worry ain't being named by white folks but being claimed by em."

"There ain't nothin we can do about that."

"We can do something about it by makin sure Jim Too learns the difference between doin somethin and lookin like he's doin somethin."

"What you tryin to say, Whisper?"

"I'm sayin, you ought a do for your own son," she said, looking at Jim Too, "what you did for that Tom Rice. At least then he'll have his own way of rememberin what you did."

It was at times like these that Jim would do whatever Whisper wanted whether he agreed with her or not. He trusted her understanding of what life gave and what it took. It had brought Jim Too into their lives and was mixed up with how she came to be called Whisper in the first place.

Whisper's mother was owned by a family who made sure to look over all the slaves working close to where they ate or slept. No slave who hadn't been checked out was allowed in the house. In the case of women, who worked in the house, they either couldn't have any more children or had agreed not to.

Whisper's mother had made that promise but got pregnant anyway. Sometime before Whisper was born, her mother was told that if the child inside her ever got in the way of her work, he or she would be sold off. From infancy, the girl was schooled in the way her mother and father would put a finger up to their lips and blow out the sound of shhhh. So the girl was taught never to raise her voice. Her folks called on her to whisper more than they called her name. After a while, what she was always called on to do took the place of her name, which after a while no one could remember.

With Whisper as a name and also something she was supposed to do, it was her mind that did the talking by raising the roof and speaking out of turn. Her mother and father told her if she didn't waste time worrying about what people thought of her, she'd have a better chance of making a life for herself.

Whisper and Jim had been together almost ten years before Jim Too crawled into their lives. They never had any children and weren't sure if Jim being partly crippled, when he was thrown from a horse years before, had anything to do with it. Jim never tried to run away but begged Whisper to leave whenever escapes were planned. She told him that going without him was out of the question. So they helped others in whatever way they could. Once during an escape in 1828, a child got separated from his family. Whisper found him wandering around the slave quarters. He looked to be about three, his body once or twice removed from the baby fat of infancy. He heaved like he was out of breath, but this stopped when he saw Whisper's long braids.

"What's your name?" she asked, leaning down. "Where's your folks?" She smiled when he didn't say anything. It took Whisper back to when she was a girl and hearing her father say that people should treat talking the same as other things the body did, doing them only when they had to and not every chance they got. "Can't you talk, boy?" she asked, with more anger than she meant.

"They told me not to," he said, thinking she was scolding him and believing it wouldn't be as bad if she knew he was under orders from people who were grown.

"I'm gonna take you home with me," she said, lifting him up in her arms.

"How come you don't have no leaves?" he asked, sliding his tiny fists over her braids.

"It ain't spring yet," Whisper said, carrying him inside the cabin.

"Where'd you find him?" Jim asked.

"Out back a ways. Whoever his people is, they won't be back."

"How you son? My name's Jim."

"I'm Jim too!" he said, happy that he'd found another Jim to go along with the mystery of Whisper's hair.

Jim Too was almost ten when Jim started teaching him to dance. And Jim was pleased no end to see how easily Jim Too took to it. Jim Too's body had the get-up of a fly, and he had to be told that the nation didn't move at the same speed as his body.

While Jim had Jim Too's body running, Whisper kept his mind moving with her talk on just about anything she saw fit to speak on. Once when they were out walking, Whisper stopped to talk to a man driving a horse and buggy. His name was Kentucky and he drove for the Churchill family. Sitting straight-backed in the buggy, he was dressed like a gentleman but the fancy clothes had the look of hand-me-downs. The horse, slavering freely, was held at bay by Kentucky's strong right arm which allowed enough slack in the reins for the horse to have the free play of its head. Watching him stirred up Whisper's flesh and had her sucking her cheeks to juice up her mouth which had gone dry.

Jim did the same thing to her. But with him, it was the pride he took in using his strength to even out the shortcomings in the rest of his body. Whisper liked that Jim was filled up enough as a person so he didn't have to live up or down to what anybody expected of him.

6

Jim Too stood beside Whisper, but couldn't catch all of what was being said between her and Kentucky. It bothered him that he was being kept out of their talk. Jim Too looked up into Whisper's face that was now being stretched by laughter. But she didn't pay him any mind, something she never did when talking to his father. When Kentucky left, Whisper didn't say anything to Jim Too about him.

"Who was that man?" he asked.

"Just a man."

"Like Daddy?"

"In some ways but not in others."

"Is he better?"

"No. Just different."

"How?"

"I don't know."

"Why don't you know?"

"Cause there're things you feel that if somebody asks you why, you couldn't tell em."

"Why not?"

"Sometimes cause you don't wanna and other times cause you can't."

"Which is it now?"

"Maybe a little of both."

"He don't look like he's so different to me."

"That's cause I'm talkin bout the way he looks to me!"

Jim Too was confused. Nothing his mother told him had ever turned out to be something he couldn't have for himself. But she didn't want to share her feelings about this man Kentucky.

The way Whisper felt about Kentucky put her in a bind because she didn't want to stop seeing him because of her life with Jim. So she decided to have both. But there were many who didn't look kindly on a woman sharing herself with more than one man....The talk began as it usually did with men during those hours away from the killing routine of work, where there was time to think, laugh, argue, and plot. But these men stopped short of using their power when it could do them the most good and took their anger out on each other.

A group of men sat in a row against the side of a barn, beat down by the day's work. Jim came out of the barn with Jim Too who sometimes worked with him. Jim Too looked forward to this get-together of men who told tales of every size and shape.

"You fellas look like you all packed and ready to jump in the ground and meet your maker," Jim said. One of the men named Ransom felt a rush of heat go through his face and was glad Jim had given him a chance to do some damage.

"As ripe as you is from shovelin hay 'n shit all day, all you'd have to do is stand over our graves and we'd be raised from the dead sooner than Jesus."

"I'm right honored, Ransom, that you think I got the power of fertilizer. I wish I could say the same for you. But I'm afraid you just smell bad."

"You wasn't listenin to me. I said you could raise the dead, because you don't seem to have much of a hold on the living."

"I got enough a one that counts with me."

"I don't know bout that. Far as I can see lately, you ain't got much of a grip on what's under your own roof."

"What's the matter with you, Ransom?" Jim said, stung by Ransom's words. "You know we never talk about each other in no family way."

"I wouldn't, cept part a your family seem to be spreadin her ways with somebody outside a you."

The other men covered up their laughter by coughing and fidgeting with their clothes. And Jim Too looked down at the ground, so he wouldn't have to meet the look coming from his father.

"I guess you gonna tell me next that it's you," Jim said, in a voice about to crack from fear. "I know you always had it strong for Whisper, but she ain't never gave you the turn of her head."

"It ain't me she turnin her head for."

"Then what you talkin bout?"

"You really don't know?"

"Know what?"

"An I thought you was just tryin to keep it on the quiet."

"Damn you, Ransom! Know what!"

Jim grabbed hold of Ransom's throat with his right hand and tightened his grip every time "Who is it?" steamed through his teeth. When the other men couldn't pull Jim's hand from Ransom's throat, they kicked and punched away at his strong side. Jim braced himself against the blows but felt his strength leaving him and then all feeling. Ransom knocked Jim's hand away which was still locked open in a choking grip. Jim Too had rushed to help his father but was held by one of the men.

"You ain't so high on the mighty side now," Ransom said, standing over Jim, swallowing hard and breathing heavy until he got his breath back. "You should a known a man in your condition couldn't hold a woman like that but for so long. Eatin your meals outa her lap ain't enough. She need a man with three legs! Damn sure wish it was me! But maybe if I wait long enough, I may get myself a turn yet. That's how you ought a look at it, Jim. As chances go round, your turn might come back again too."

"Who is it?" Jim said, in a voice sizzling around the edges.

"Why don't you ask your son?"

Jim watched the overalls stretching up above him crack at the knees as Ransom and the other men left him lying on the ground. Jim didn't try to get up right away. He wanted to relax and not feel anything for as long as possible. It was a relief from the battle between the dead weight of his left side and the mus-cled-up strength of his right. When the feeling in his right side came back, it was pain.

Jim Too still couldn't look at his father. He'd watched those men beat him; and now that Jim knew about this other man, there was no way for Jim Too to say anything without hurting both his father and mother.

9

"Who is he?" Jim asked, without much behind it.

"Just somebody she talk to."

"I ain't asked you that."

"I don't know his name. He drive a buggy all the time."

Jim waited until after Jim Too went to bed that night before talking with Whisper.

"Who's the man you been talkin to?"

Her stomach gave way as she tried to act like she had nothing to hide.

"Why you ask?"

"I thought it was about time."

"His name's Kentucky."

"That buggy driver for Churchill?"

"That's him."

"Your name came up in some talk about him. And I wanna know if it belongs there. Cause if it don't, I'll put a stop to it— the next person I hear talkin your name into places where it ain't got no business."

"What people been sayin?"

"That you and him talk pretty regular."

"That's true."

"But that ain't all of it. They say the talkin you doin ain't just with words. It's like you sayin 'how you do' with your mouth but your eyes is on speakin terms with his flesh."

"Thinkin ain't doin, Jim."

"It is if that's what you thinkin when you doin it with me."

"There ain't nobody in the way when I'm with you."

"Which half a me you talkin bout?"

"I ain't never thought a you as half a anything."

"Well, who do you wanna be with? Him or me?"

"I wanna be with you but you can't have all a me."

"That mean you still gonna carry on with that well-hung buck?"

"Bein in his company don't mean I'm in his pants."

"Maybe not yet it don't."

"That's in your head, not mine."

"What you doin ain't proper for a woman."

"I think I got somethin to say about that."

"I guess next you gonna tell me you ain't no slave."

"Only by law. And that's somethin I learnt from you, Jim. When you dance ain't nobody got a claim on you. Ain't that what you told that white man, Rice? That there was things in you he couldn't have, even if you wanted to give em to him. That's all I'm sayin, Jim."

Jim leaned forward in his rocker and touched her like he was trying to find his way in the dark.

"Don't see him no more," he said softly.

"I can't do that, Jim."

Jim sat back in his rocker.

"There's a lot a right in what you say, Whisper. But I can't use it no more. Ever since that day I got throwed by that horse, there ain't been no way I could get away from knowin that half a me wasn't ever gonna move again. So I tried to make up for it by makin my other half do things so good I'd forget about the rest a me. But that ain't never happened. And the thing is, now I'm glad that's the way it is cause I need to know there's some things in my life that ain't gonna move, that I know gonna be the same all the time....You too much in the world, Whisper. And I can't keep up with you no more. There don't seem to be nothin bout you that don't move. And the way I am now, I need a part a you to be still, not to move, not to wanna be in two places at once. I'm tired a turnin my head and findin you done moved again. So if you can't find it anywhere in yourself to be still for me in the way I want, don't say anything. Just leave. And do it now! Cause if you don't, I'll stop you from movin for good!"

Whisper left that same night and moved in with a woman she knew in another section of the Quarters. Jim Too stayed with Jim but spent as much time with Whisper as he ever had. They told him what happened between them, but it didn't make Jim Too feel any better. For some reason, Jim and Whisper could do what they wanted whether he liked it or not. Jim Too couldn't say to either one of them what Whisper had said to Jim. He couldn't tell them what to do like Jim had done to Whisper. And he couldn't leave because his only memory of leaving was with grown-ups—which ended with his being lost and found again by somebody grown. Jim Too wondered if all this had something to do with a word he'd heard blacks use when talking among themselves. And it came as a surprise to him when he started hearing the same word—FREE—used whenever he danced.

A minstrel show came through Louisville ten years later. The main attraction was a dancer named Jack Diamond who was said to be a master of the jig and the breakdown. Over the years, Jim Too had caused quite a buzz of his own around Louisville for his dancing at white social functions. And there was talk of a contest between the two.

One night a carriage pulled up in front of one of the cabins in the Quarters. The driver stepped down and helped his passenger off. He was a man with thick white hair over his eyes and down both sides of his face. With the help of a knobby cane, he made his way to the cabin and knocked once on the door with the head of the cane.

"Evenin Jim," the man said, when the door opened.

"Mister Churchill."

"I have somethin I wanna talk over with you."

He walked slowly into the cabin and sat down in the rocker. "Where's Jim Too? What I wanna talk about concerns him."

"He's visitin with his mother."

"Well, you probably heard about the show comin through here with that dancer, Jack Diamond....I wanna set up a contest between him and Jim Too. And I want you to get him ready for it. If he wins, it could mean a chance to dance in a travelin show. Jim Too could be the first Negro in a white minstrel show."

Jim only half-listened to what Churchill said. The rest of his attention was on the driver, framed by the window, leaning against the buggy.

"There's somethin I want too, Mister Churchill."

"I won't free you, Jim."

"Don't worry, Mister Churchill. That's somethin I won't ever ask you for."

13

"What do you want then?"

"It's your driver, Kentucky."

"What about him?"

"I want you to sell him off."

Churchill couldn't believe what Jim had said, but his surprise didn't last long.

"Oh! So that's it. I'd forgotten all about that."

"That's what I want Mister Churchill, for me to do what you want."

"Kentucky's been with me a long time."

"Maybe you can visit him sometime."

The tone of Jim's voice told Churchill how stupid his own words must have sounded.

"You're quite a character. You know that?"

"No I'm not. I'm just somebody who wants to trade you for somethin you want."

"You know this won't get her back?"

"I don't want her back. I want him gone!"

"You know, Jim, this is quite a surprise and somewhat of a disappointment. I've always rated you a cut above the run-of-the-mill nigger or even white, for that matter. I figured you for better than this."

"Right now, I don't wanna be better than this."

Churchill looked at Jim Crow and stretched his right leg out, which started to ache from arthritis. But it didn't take him long to figure out that the pain in his knee wasn't bothering him as much as what Jim had said. Churchill knew that, even with his high standing as a property-owning white man, there were blacks made of tougher leather than he was. But what he needed to keep them in their place was his belief that he always knew what they were up to. Now here was a black telling him: "I'm no better than you, not because I can't be, but because I don't wanna be." This was hard for Churchill to swallow because it was easier to lord it over or suck up to people than to face them as an equal. Churchill had to smile at how well Jim had read him. He would sell Kentucky because his pride needed Jim Too's talent for dancing more than he needed a buggy driver.

Jim stood in the doorway and watched Kentucky help Churchill into the buggy. Kentucky turned to climb up into the driver's seat. His eyes met Jim's, holding what they both knew and what one of them didn't know.

On the morning of the contest between Jim Too and Jack Diamond, some black men started building a platform on the grounds outside the Churchill mansion. They hammered nail after nail into the wood and soon their naked bodies from the waist up took on a sweat shine.

People started arriving around noon. The area closest to the platform was taken up by property-owning whites who knew the Churchills socially. Behind them were whites whose lot in life was only a skin color away from the slavery of blacks who were the farthest away from the platform. But as the excitement leading up to the contest started to build, it was hard for people to stay where they belonged.

The betting started out between white men over who was the more thoroughbred of the two dancers. They put their hands alongside their mouths and whispered to black men who were supposed to have the inside track on what odds to lay down. Trying to find out who was in the know soon carried over into joking, long, tall tales, and outright lying. But the knack for telling a good story caused whites to joke about how expecting blacks to speak a word of truth was as likely to happen as believing they could give you an honest day's work.

Black and white women mixed it up with the men, giving more than a good account of themselves with their own ideas on which of the two dancers would win. They did this while unpacking baskets of food and watching out for children who were often not their own or their color.

In the middle of all this, the black men relaxed on the platform. None of them saw Jim Too when he slipped underneath the platform. Jim had always told him to stay out of sight on the day of a match. Since people expected Jim Too to do the impossible, Jim didn't want him seen before the contest doing anything plain and simple. He told Jim Too that it was important to show people he was different from them but not better. And there'd been many times over the years when Jim Too showed everybody how different he was.

Jim Too had grown into a muscled-up young man with a body toughened by working in the fields. But it was his heavy-lidded, sorrow-filled eyes that made people think there was something not quite right about him even before he danced his first step. These were the eyes that had stared down Tom Rice and anybody else who got in their way. Most people were of the opinion that Jim Too's eyes could hold all that sadness in them because there was a lot more inside him than just his own life. When he started dancing, it was a relief to those who couldn't look into his eyes for very long. It was the one thing he did that people couldn't stop looking at.

Jim Too stretched his arms and legs; he then sat very still and listened to the talk of the men above him.

"When'd it happen?" one of the men asked.

"This morning bout the time we started work on this platform," another said. "Churchill fetched him from Whisper's place."

"How'd he know to look for him there?"

"It ain't no secret. Everybody includin Kentucky's woman know he spend a couple days out the week at Whisper's....Anyway, Churchill and Kentucky is out on the road in this buggy when they come up on four mangy lookin white men on horseback who blockin the road. One of em talking through a mouth that looks like it's full a horseshit says, 'You'll be comin with us now, Kentucky.' Kentucky turns around in the buggy to ask Churchill what's goin on, but before Kentucky can say somethin, he's hit in the head and knocked to the ground.

"They all around him when he gets to his feet. But Kentucky don't pay em no mind or the blood the color of axle grease leakin out a hole in the back of his head. He got his eyes fixed on Churchill sittin in the buggy and he says, 'Why you doin this, Mister Churchill?' But Churchill don't say nothin. Then the man with the mouth full a manure says, 'Let's go coonskin!' They try to get a hold a him but he knocks them away like he's shooin flies. When the two of em come at him with a whip, Kentucky braces himself and catches one whip high up on his arm and the other around his waist. But he's so strong, he yanks both the men at the end of the whips off their feet and locks their heads under his arms. The other two men point they rifles at him but Churchill raises his hand for them to stop, looks at Kentucky and says—

"'I don't have to explain a thing.'

"'I know but I wanna know anyway,' Kentucky says.

"'I made a deal with Jim Crow. He wanted you sold off in exchange for him agreein to get Jim Too ready for the contest with Jack Diamond.'

"When Kentucky hears that, his face starts to change. It's like he was turnin something over in his mind that was also happenin on his face. Then he gets this devilish grin on his mouth; he starts laughin and holdin those two men who look like they growin right out his underarms, while the other two still got they rifles pointed at him.

"'Release those two men at once!' Churchill says.

"'Don't worry, I aim to. But from the trouble and sufferin of this world.'

"'Now you listen to me!'

"'I heard you the first time. You made a deal with a slave to sell another slave, somethin you never needed no help doin before. I was born into a deal I never had no say in. But I'm a have some say in this one.'

"'I would a sent your family wherever you were, includin your other woman, if that's what you wanted.'

"'Just how was you gonna find out what I wanted? The way you goin about it now?'

"'I didn't want it this way but this is the way it is. Now I'm only gonna ask you once more. Let those men go!'

"'Not if I gotta pay the same price whether I let em go or not.'

"'Damn you, Kentucky!'

"Churchill keeps saying that and poundin his fist into the seat of the buggy. Then he quiets down, looks at the two pointin they rifles at Kentucky and says, 'All right you two, finish him!'

"'If they shoot, there gonna be two broke-neck peckerwoods before I hit the ground,' Kentucky says. They keep still for a second or two, then raise the gun barrels and let both rifle butts touch the ground.

"'We can't do it, not just yet anyway,' one says. 'It's been too many years and a lot a beers with these two. Let him go, Mister Churchill. He won't get far. He wants to live; and so long as they live, he lives.'

"'All right, Kentucky. What's it gonna be?' Churchill says.

"'It's gonna be me walkin north with these two till I get clear. Anybody tryin to stop me before then and I break these two in half at the neck bone.'

"So they let Kentucky walk off with those two bounty hunters under his arms. And from a distance, the three of em looks like some giant six-legged spider. My guess is that if Kentucky ain't caught and keeps followin the drinkin gourd, he'll end up in freedom one a these days."

The other men were so caught up in the story they couldn't speak. At the same time the foglike quiet came down on them, Jim Too felt his body jerking. The anger at Jim and Whisper for tearing them apart was still in him. And while Jim Too never let himself get close to Kentucky, what the storyteller said bothered him.

"You makin Kentucky out to be more than he is," a man said, finally.

"What you think he is?"

"A slave."

"He's more than that even if everything didn't happen just like I said."

"But if you wasn't there, how you know any of it's true? From what I heard, Kentucky was killed tryin to escape."

"I'll tell you what. You tell what you heard and I'll keep spreadin what I just told you. And we'll see in a year from now which story folks'll remember, yours or mine. None of us probably ever gonna see Kentucky again. So I figure my story's as good or better than anything we gonna hear. If you ain't satisfied, you can always go ask Churchill what happened. I know he'll be glad to tell you."

Different stories of what happened to Kentucky were heard all day. By the time the daylight was smeared with night, there was more talk about what happened to Kentucky than about the contest between Jim Too and Jack Diamond. But like the storyteller who helped build the platform said, his story was the one most people believed. And even whites, who didn't believe a word of it, couldn't help but listen no matter how many times they heard it.

Tom Rice watched Jack Diamond put on his boots in one of the guest rooms in the Churchill mansion. Diamond seemed to get a lot of pleasure out of something that didn't amount to much. Rice remembered the time when he got enjoyment out of the smallest things. But all that changed when Jim Crow told him all he did was copy other people....When Rice was in his room that night, he wiped the burnt cork off his face and stared at the black smudge in the towel. He'd started using it in the 1820s when slave revolts were on the rise. White faces covered with burnt cork gave the newborn settlements a black face that was much easier on the eyes. Rice understood this and gave people what they wanted. But there was something else that made him blacken his face. It had to do with a hunger for things belonging to other people.

When Rice was growing up, he went from taking anything that was lying around to making himself out to be anybody he found interesting. Once when a traveling show came through Philadelphia, Rice was surprised to find out that an actor playing the role of a man over seventy was only twenty. After the show left town, Rice stowed away in a wagon. He was found too far out on the road for them to take him back; and by the time they reached the next town, Rice had wormed his way into everyone's heart.

Rice moved quickly from doing the dirty work that was part of a traveling show to becoming a fullfledged actor. In his first role, he played the part of a newcomer, staking his fortune on the frontier. Rice got a stranger to let him borrow his buckskins for the show. But in the middle of the scene, the man's voice was heard offstage.

"Hurry up with my things or else it's gonna cost you extra!"

The man kept yelling until, fed up, Rice took off the buckskins, threw them offstage and finished the performance in his long underwear. He told the audience he was dressed just like the frontier—which was a territory still in its undies that had just woke up. The audience loved it and the skit became a regular part of the show.

Rice played characters like Daniel Boone, Davy Crockett, and Andrew Jackson who always came to mind whenever people thought about the frontier spirit. It wasn't long before he added Indians and blacks to his list of characters and used them as dramatic fodder to be conquered by the likes of Boone, Crockett, and Jackson.

Rice had spent his life getting inside the skin of other people. But his belief in himself was shaken when Jim Crow told him he wasn't even good at faking it....That night Rice took a piece of burnt cork and smeared it back on his face. He grabbed a handful of dirt from a sack he always had with him and rubbed it into his arms, chest, and legs. He then put on pieces of different getups he wore in his act. He got into bed and pulled the covers up to his neck. He admitted it. He was a scavenger: but one of a special breed who stole only the things people couldn't get rid of. Rice lay in bed and waited for the next person to ask him to give back the parts of themselves that he'd taken to make himself feel alive.

Rice didn't get out of bed until the show the next night. And the other members of the company had to beg him to go on. Acting was no longer enough to get Rice through the hours when the only make-up he wore was his own face. And it was years before that would change.

"It ever bother you," Rice finally said, "all this dancin the darky business?"

"No. Why should it?" Diamond said. "It's what I like doin."

"But don't it bother you sometimes that most of the time you make believe you somebody else?"

"I don't think about it. Even when I ain't dancin, I'm still makin things up. The only difference is—when I'm on stage, I'm tryin to make a believer out a more people than just me."

"You remember what I told you about comin through here years ago and meetin Jim Crow, the father of the fella you hoofin up against tonight? Well, he taught me this dance that I started usin in my act. It went over big with the audience, but when I told him about it, he damn near accused me of stealin it from him."

"Was he right?" Diamond asked.

"He wasn't in no position to judge me. He never even saw me do it!"

"But you were there. You know what you did."

"I thought I did. But I quit performin for a long time after that."

"Well, whatever you was doin, you must a been pretty good at it. From what I heard, you was one of the best: an all-around trouper. I figure there must a been somethin bonafide about you, for you to convince people you was doin something worth payin attention to."

"Maybe so. But it's just that I was never spoke to like that by a black before."

"It might a been the first time for him too."

"What do you mean?"

"Well, when he showed you that dance, he was more than just some broken-down nigger slave. And once you allow somebody to be more than one thing at a time, ain't nothin nailed down no more, includin you!"

"So you sayin it won't bother you if you get beat out by this Jim Too?"

"Course it'll bother me. But I'll get over it like I'm gonna get over life when I finally kick out....But before that happens, I hope I live to see the day when I can benefit from blacks more than I do now. Since I ain't never gonna own nobody like Churchill does, I'd rather see blacks with as much say-so in the world as I got. That way it'd be easier for me to take advantage of what they got to offer. Course, if that happens, it goes without sayin that I'd have to accept that they'd be tryin to take fair and unfair advantage of me too."

"You a hard person to figure," Rice said.

"That shouldn't surprise you, much as you've seen me dance."

Churchill had watched Kentucky disappear in the distance with the two men hanging under his arms like bladders. The other two bounty hunters took out after them as soon as they were out of sight. Churchill turned the buggy around, drove back to the mansion, went to his room, locked the door, and didn't move for hours. When he did get up from his chair, he went to the guest room where Rice and Diamond were staying.

"I just wanted to make sure everything was all right," he said, when Rice opened the door. "I'm sorry I haven't been a more gracious host, but one of my slaves ran off early this morning and I've had to direct all my attention to that."

"Was he caught?" Rice asked.

"No, but he will be, one way or the other."

"He isn't a dancer, is he?" Diamond asked.

"Not to my knowledge. He's been my personal driver for years."

"Are you surprised he run off?"

"There were some circumstances leading to his escape that I don't care to go into."

"Something other than wanting to be free?"

"I'd rather not go into it, Mister Diamond."

"I don't want to pry into your affairs, Mister Churchill," Rice said, "but with all that's already happened today, a dance contest might be the last thing you'd want."

"On the contrary, I'd rather have attention focused on dancing than an escape. And if Jim Too beats Diamond here, it'll be all to the good, cause the celebration will be the result of someone who's still here and not someone who's run off."

"I can appreciate your reasoning, Mister Churchill, but have you considered the possibility that a contest like this could be an

24

inspiration for other blacks to escape?"

"You can't be serious?"

"I am. But I can understand someone in your position not thinking much of the effect a dancer the caliber of Jim Too could have on other blacks."

"I'm well aware of what someone with Jim Too's ability is capable of. And I've made plans for him beyond this evening's contest with that in mind. It wouldn't be, Mister Rice, that you have second thoughts about Diamond competing against Jim Too? In which case, you would forfeit your bet."

"You're right," Diamond said, standing up, "You know your business a lot better than we do."

He then went into a quick step that looked as if he wasn't bending his knees or lifting his feet off the floor. After a while, the sound of his boots against the floor got softer and softer until all that could be heard was a tapping like fingertips on a table.

Whisper found out about Kentucky when she overheard some women talking on the grounds near the platform. Her body went stiff as a stick and she didn't move until a woman she knew spoke to her.

"I don't know if you heard ..."

"I did."

"You hear about Jim's part in it?"

"I don't know if I want to."

"You want me to stop?"

"You didn't ask me if you could start."

"It's goin around that Kentucky was sold off as part of a deal Churchill made with Jim to get Jim Too ready for the match with Jack Diamond. When Kentucky got wind of it, he took off."

"Sounds like there's a man goin round takin names and fixin blame," Whisper said. "But since Kentucky can't answer for himself and Churchill don't have to, that only leaves Jim."

"You don't think he's gonna admit it, do you?"

"He will if it's true."

Whisper hadn't been back to the cabin she shared with Jim and Jim Too since the night ten years before when Jim told her to get out. There were times when they were close enough to speak, but no words ever passed between them. What Whisper heard about Jim usually came from Jim Too when he came to stay with her.

When Whisper first heard about Kentucky running off, she felt anger. That was always the first thing she felt when she was scared or hurt. And it was anger that pushed her to go to Jim's cabin. But she knew Kentucky was gone out of her life no matter who was to blame. While Whisper walked, sweat broke out on her forehead and she started getting dizzy. She fell to her knees and threw up. It took a while before her stomach settled enough for her to go on.

Right before Whisper knocked on Jim's cabin door, she had the feeling that there were other people around, hiding in the dark.

"Come on," Jim said from behind the door. Jim had his back to her when she walked in. He dragged his left leg as he turned around.

"Whisper."

"Is it true what's goin round bout your part in getting Kentucky sold off?"

"Pretty much."

She was glad they hadn't talked around the edges of it.

"Where's Jim Too?" she asked.

"He's limberin up over by the platform."

"I remember years ago you said the only thing worse than bein treated wrong was givin yourself the treatment without no help."

"I don't believe that no more," Jim said. "For better or worse, I want what happens to me to be my own doin."

"What happened to Kentucky wasn't HIS doin! It was yours and Churchill's!"

"You right. But gettin away was his doin. And that's what freedom's all about."

"You think what you did to Kentucky makes you free?"

"Why not? I know it hurt some people. But that's what I wanted to do! Slavery helped but slavery didn't do it. I did! And like it or not, that's a kind a freedom we gonna have long after this slavery is over."

There was no more anger in Whisper, just a fear that Jim might be right. What he'd done had turned her stomach, but she was just as upset that he didn't seem bothered by it.

"When we was together," she finally said, "I never thought a you as crippled. You favored a leg like you favored life, always fig-urin out ways to make it do things nobody would a thought possible. But you crippled now like you never was before, even with the full use of only half your body. Doin something just cause you can don't make you free. Bein free is doin somethin cause you have to! Cause your life depends on it! What you did ain't got nothin to do with that. Your life didn't depend on it. But Kentucky's did! The freedom I'm talkin bout don't keep company with the low, spiteful thing you did. Face it. You did it cause you could get away with it! All you proved was that you can lie down with the worst of what white folks do. And that ain't somethin I'd want a reputation for....Maybe your life does depend on what you call freedom, after all. But I doubt if you gonna feel much like dancin anymore, much less be able to."

"If you finished with what you come over here for," Jim said, "I'll be gettin over to see bout Jim Too."

"I think you ought a know, there's some men layin for you outside."

"Thanks for the warning, but they a little late."

As soon as they were out the door, men came out from the cover of darkness with anger rattling in their bones. Jim walked over to them. His left leg dragged and made a scraping sound on the ground. He stopped close enough to see there were six of them. But it was too dark to see any of their faces.

"I guess all a you bein here means you heard I had a hand in what happened to Kentucky. Well, it's true but you too late to do me much harm cause I'm already done in. About the only thing I'm fit to do now is watch my son do what I ain't no more good for. Now you can stop me from even doin that if you want. But if you do, it won't be no different from what I did cause you ain't riskin nothin....Whatever I did don't happen 'less Churchill go along with it. I'm easy. But what about him? Can you jump out the shadows for him like you doin for me? Now, I'm either gonna die right here in the dirt or I'm goin over to where Jim Too is and see if he can jig me through whatever life I got left!"

Jim dragged his way closer to them and they stepped aside. If there had been even the smallest sign that Jim was trying to talk his way out of what he'd done, they would've killed him right there. But he came out of his mouth with words that had those men thinking more about what they were going to do than what he'd already done. And so Jim took his life out of their hands and put it back in his own. Would you look at that! Whisper thought. He wasn't dancing but he was still kicking!

Lanterns were hung and hand-held around the platform. The crowd seemed to breathe as one person as it got closer to the start of the contest. White men stood around with cigars in their mouths and their chests sticking out. Jim and Jim Too were sitting underneath the platform and could only see the legs of people getting riled up from having to wait so long. Jim watched Jim Too stretch his arms and legs. He tried to remember when the softness of his son's face had started to give way to the harder look of a man. The fact that Jim Too had gotten mannish was something Jim wouldn't have given a lot of thought to. But the contest between Jim Too and Jack Diamond gave Jim reason to hope that fate had something in store for his son other than slavery.

"Why you wanna talk under here?" Jim Too asked.

"I just want you to have one more look at folks from where their walkin goes on before you get out there and dance. Everything I've tried to teach you comes out a the way every creature on this earth gets around—whether on all fours or upright. All these upright folks is here cause you can leg it out with the best that's ever done it. And you make em feel better about the way they get around, especially if they ain't feelin so upstandin."

"Is that how you feelin right now?"

"Why you say that?"

"Cause I heard what happened to Kentucky and I talked to Mama."

"What she tell you?"

"She told me to talk to you."

"Your mother's got her own understandin of what happened—which is all right by me cause I got mine."

30

"Did you do it?" Jim Too asked.

"I'll talk to you bout it after the match."

"I wanna know now."

"I told Churchill what I wanted him to do. But I didn't make him do it."

"No. But you used me to get him to do it. When you told Mama to leave, you left me out of it. And now, when you wanna get rid a Kentucky, you put me in it. When you gonna stop makin me part a things I never have no say in?"

"I got a feelin this may be the last time. Course, I can't speak for nobody else."

"Yeah, nobody except me!" Jim Too said.

A breath of laughter jumped out of Jim's mouth. He crawled to the edge of the platform. But before getting out from underneath it, he turned back to Jim Too.

"In case you forgot, whatever plans I had in mind for you is the least a your worries."

A white man who'd been talking with Churchill near the platform climbed up onto it and raised his arms to get everybody to quiet down.

"May I have your attention, please! We about ready to start," he said.

When the crowd didn't stop talking right away, the man frowned. But he took a deep breath and started again.

"What we got here tonight is what happens when legs outgrow the britches that walkin is made from and runnin becomes new duds for the legs."

The crowd quieted down some; and seeing that he'd gotten people to listen, the man wasn't about to let them get away.

"As you all know, in a contest like this, the idea is for both dancers to take turns tryin to top each other till one of em can't do what's called for....So now that you've heard the guts of it, let's get on with the whole hog! The first one to play the platform with a dance is Jack Diamond who makes a stage out a anything comin underneath his feet."

Jack Diamond was heard before he was seen with the quick taps of his boots against the steps leading up to the platform. The sight of him got whoops and hollers from the crowd.

"And now, the other half of this heel and toe showdown," the man said, "one of our own who's been kickin up his heels where his daddy left off. Jim Too Crow!"

From the other side of the platform, Jim Too high-stepped his way up the ladder, squatted, and placed his hands flat on the wooden floor. He leaned forward, pressed his elbows against his thighs, and lifted himself into a handstand. His pant legs dropped down around his calves as he walked on his hands to the front of the platform. Jim Too then lowered his legs at an angle with the rest of his body and flipped himself up onto his feet.

"All right, you two don't need me to jump in the jaws no more," the man yelled. But his voice was just about drowned out by the cheers and whistles from the crowd. He then pointed at Jack Diamond to begin.

Diamond's boots were a blanket of footprints as they hammered into the floor. He gave up the floor to Jim Too who copied him step for step and followed that up by squatting with his arms folded and kicking his legs out side to side. They swapped moves like they were stories, telling each other things with their body talk that they couldn't put into words.

The cheering and screaming from the crowd went back and forth between favoring one of them and then the other. After almost an hour, Jim Too felt his body getting away from him. And then while in the middle of a quick stomping jig, he started clapping his hands against his arms, chest, thighs, and each other. People who'd been whooping it up got quiet and looked like they were watching someone having a breakdown. Diamond stopped dancing and stood with his mouth open.

And then it happened. Blacks were the first to move as though they'd been given a signal from Jim Too. Women yanked at the arms of their children, pulling them away from the platform, and running into the darkness of the night. White men who tried to stop them were beaten back by rocks and sticks. Other black women and men didn't run but attacked whites and blacks who'd done them wrong in the past. Some white women were strangled with their own hair. Picks and shovels that had been used earlier in the day to dig up the earth were now cutting into flesh. It was like the world had been turned inside out and the bones were a cage around the meat inside.

Blacks weren't the only ones getting even with people who'd hurt them. A white woman stabbed a man between his shoulder blades with a knitting needle. Two children cried as they watched the man jerking with the needle poking out of his back. Some people didn't run or try to settle old scores. They just walked away. One woman untied her reddish-brown hair, opened her dress, and undid her underclothes. When her petticoat and corset dropped to the ground, she walked straight ahead and got lost in the darkness.

It took some time, but finally blacks and whites, who stood around like they were frozen, started to thaw out. They put hammerlocks on people who tried to run or beat up on others. Some men wrestled Jim Too down on the platform and carried him twisting and kicking into the Churchill mansion. By the next morning, most of the fight had been taken out of people, and armed white men stood guard on the grounds surrounding the mansion.

Churchill and slaveowners from nearby plantations were seated in his parlor. They were all shaken up by what had happened and seemed to be waiting for Churchill to tell them that the bottom of the world had not fallen through the top.

"What are we gonna do?" one of the men asked.

"We have to do something. But it has to be the right thing," Churchill said.

"What do you have in mind?" another man asked.

"To do everything we can to destroy all evidence of what happened here."

"What do you mean?"

"That's not possible! The blacks will never forget this!"

"They will," Churchill said, "if we make it difficult for them to keep their memory of it alive."

"How do we do that?"

"We send bounty hunters after those who've escaped with orders to kill everyone they capture."

"That include children?"

"Of course! Unless you want children back here who'll grow up with the memory of their kinfolk being murdered on your say-so."

"What else?"

"We sell off anyone who had family escape and anybody else who we suspect will give us trouble."

"What about Jim Too? He's the one who started it all."

"I have something planned for him," Churchill said, "that'll guarantee he doesn't become a martyr."

Churchill didn't say anymore about what he planned to do but promised the other men in the room that Jim Too's dancing would never get out of hand again. The next day Jim Too was taken under guard to a storage barn on the plantation grounds. Whisper and Jim were already there when he was brought in. They both tried to go to him but were held back by the men around them. Jim Too looked at his mother and father and his eyes burned with fear. Churchill walked into the barn with two men on each side of him. He didn't speak but stared at the three of them. He didn't seem to be in any hurry.

"All this trouble started with you three," Churchill said. "And I'm gonna make sure it ends with you."

He looked at Jim.

"You'll be stayin. But not you," he said turning to Whisper and then to Jim Too. "You're goin with Tom Rice's travelin show....And if you should get it in your head to run off, Rice'll get word to me and you can forget about ever seein either one of them again. If you got any goodbyes you wanna say, you better say em now."

Churchill nodded his head for the men to let Jim Too go. But he didn't rush to his mother or father. It was happening again, he thought. The first time, Whisper and Jim had pulled them apart. And now Churchill was doing it. Jim Too walked slowly over to Whisper. When he got to her, he touched the side of her face with the palm of his hand, closed his fingers around one of her braids, and slid his hand all the way down the roped hair. Whisper pressed the side of her head against his chest like she wanted to remember his heartbeat. They she spoke into his chest; and Jim Too not only heard her voice but felt the words in her breath.

"Remember what I used to tell you when you got scared?"

"Every goodbye ain't gone. All sickness ain't death. And every big man ain't strong," he said.

Whisper pushed away from Jim Too and pulled her arms back when he tried to reach for her. She turned back for one more look at him as the men took her out.

Jim Too turned around to face his father.

"Why they doin this?" he asked, choking up and rubbing his eyes with the back of his hand.

"They don't wanna believe what happened; so they gonna get rid of everything that reminds em of it."

"How come they ain't gettin get rid a you?"

"I guess I don't worry them as much as you and Whisper."

"I see why they feel that way."

"I'm a tell you somethin. Don't spend your life runnin me into the ground. Take what you can use from whatever I gave you and let the rest go. It ain't for my sake I'm tellin you this. It's for yours."

"Finish it up!" Churchill said.

"You'll be all right," Jim said, "Just do what you're told. But don't tell what you know."

"I'm a tell you somethin I know. I ain't never gonna answer to Jim Too no more! I don't want no name that sounds like I'm the same as you!"

Jim Too watched his father crack and come apart from all the hurt that was in those words. But Jim held himself together and started doing every move his body could remember. And as he stamped it all down into the ground, the juice in his legs turned muddy. He knew then that his body could no longer take him past what he was doing to become what he was doing.

Churchill nodded to one of the men next to Jim Too. A slab of hand fell on his shoulder and he was taken out. Churchill then told the other men to wait outside so he could talk to Jim alone.

"Jim. I want you to know something."

"I already know, Mister Churchill. I watched you do it. For a while there I didn't know if you had it in you."

"Had what in me?"

"What it takes to bring the worse out a you. With Kentucky, you needed my help. But this time, you did it all by yourself."

Churchill raised his cane but Jim snatched it away from him.

"You dropped your cane, Mister Churchill. You gotta be more careful."

"You're right. And you just helped me with something that'll make me feel a lot better about getting rid of you. Now nigger, gimme that cane!"

Churchill held out his hand but his eyes got big as silver dollars when he saw Jim raise the cane to hit him.

Tom Rice and Jack Diamond were waiting for Jim Too at the Louisville train station as he was led in, tied across a horse like a bedroll, in the company of two bounty hunters. After Jim Too was untied and turned over to Rice, the three of them got on the train and entered the car filled with the other members of the traveling show. Their faces twisted up when they saw Jim Too, and they all got up and left the car without saying a word.

"Well, I guess from now on, this here's the Jim Crow car," Jim Too said.

"You the one everybody's gonna be comin to see. You ought a have your own car," Diamond said.

"What they comin to see me for?"

"A lot a people heard about you," Rice said. "And they wanna get a better look."

"What they wanna look at?"

"Your dancin."

"I didn't know white folks was interested in seein anybody colored in a minstrel show unless they was white folks actin like they colored."

"Once they see you dance, that won't be true no more," Rice said.

"Mister Rice, ain't you a dancer too?" Jim Too asked.

"I can dance. But I'm not a dancer....Look, Jim Too ..."

"My name's Jim!"

"All right. Jim....Let me set you straight on a few things. This travelin show is my life. And it's the only life I want. I know the life you got and the life you want ain't the same like it is for me. But it's a damn sight better than it would be if you was back slavin for Churchill. You need to think about that, if you get the itch to run off. I'm no bounty hunter. So I can't stop you or chase after you if you run off. The only thing that concerns me is that with you and Jack in the show, I got somethin no other minstrel show's got. And if you stay, what you got is the chance to do somethin you wanna do—which ain't the case for most colored folks!"

The first time Jim danced with Tom Rice's Non-Pareil Minstrel Show was outdoors in a clearing of some Kentucky woods that looked like it had been shaved clean with a razor. A platform was set up and people started arriving hours before the show got going. They slaughtered pigs, started cooking fires, and kept themselves in stitches with spicy talk and jokes. Rice told Jim to stay in one of the covered wagons until showtime, just in case there were people who wouldn't look kindly on a black man acting footloose and free when he wasn't on stage.

When the show was about to start, the air was thick with the smell of barbequed pork and corn liquor. Whistling punched holes in the night air and the foot stomping was louder than a herd of stampeding cattle. Finally, one of the actors walked to the center of the stage.

"Tonight, we startin the show off with the story of that legendary Kentucky backwoodsman, second in notoriety only to Daniel Boone. Ladies and Gents: Daniel Bones!"

A man shuffled onto the stage with burnt cork smeared over his whole face except for his lips, which were painted white. His eyes bugged and stared out of the darkness of his face. The crowd shook with laughter at the sight of him. The man pointed to himself and acted like he didn't understand why people were laughing at him. Then he lifted his shoulders and took a bow.

"That's me," he said. "Bones! Daniel Bones! Kentucky's first and most dutiful son....Yes I am I am. Think on it a minute. Everybody here is skin and bones. But what comes first?"

He cupped his hand over his ear.

"Bones!" the crowd yelled.

"That's me!" he cried out. "I told you! Bones! Daniel Bones!"

The crowd slapped their knees, buckled in at the waist, and nodded their heads at one another. But then the man's banana-shaped smile bent slowly into a frown that turned him into a sack of woe. The audience got quiet again.

"But I don't unnerstan you folks at all. Cause you don't pay no mind to what comes first, only to what comes second. I know skin is like next a kin. But it's bones that get you through what's thick and thin! Am I right or wrong?"

"Right!" the crowd shouted back.

The man shook his head slowly.

"Y'all still don't know me, do you? I'm Bones! Which only shows to go you that when I'm right, nobody listens. And when I'm wrong, nobody cares. But I'm not gonna get no ways weary cause I'm Kentucky's first and most dutiful son, secure in the knowledge that when God was studyin on makin the human race, he wasn't studyin on Adam's skin but his ribs. So you can stick with the skin if you wanna. But I'm a stick with the ribs!"

People were all inside and beside themselves with laughter as Bones's mouth curled up in a grin from ear to ear. He then slipped and nearly fell on his way off the stage. But before going down the foot ladder, he stopped and put his finger up to his mouth to make the crowd be silent.

"What comes first?" he called out again and cupped his hand over his ear.

"Bones!" they yelled and said it over and over again like they'd just gotten good religion. Bones lifted his hands again for quiet.

"You're right! And I may be right too cause I'm Bones for sure. But you can be Bones too if you'd get up off your skin like me. Cause I'm the beginning, the middle, and the end a life. And if you don't think that's the God's honest truth, just mosey on over to all the throwaway from the barbeque you been chewin on today and see what you find. Bones! That's me! I'm everywhere you look!"

And then he was gone, as quick as he'd been slow to show

himself. The crowd was on its feet, clapping with added helpings of hollers and whistles. Jim watched the actor disappear into the shadows below the stage. Then someone lit a lantern and as the glow from the flame spread inside the glass, there was the face of Thomas Rice!

The show went on and Jim couldn't take his eyes off the actors as they tried to get the best of each other by slugging it out with words or through fancy footwork. There were other skits like the one on Daniel Bones and short plays where actors in black face combed their hair with a wagon wheel and washed up in a skillet that made them white again. At different points in the show, actors broke into song and dance and played bone clappers, tambourines, and banjos.

During the intermission, Jim limbered up behind bedsheets strung across a rope rigged up between two trees near the edge of the clearing.

"You ready?" Rice asked.

"I reckon I'm about to find out."

"Remember in the finale, you and Jack face off for a dance to the finish. The idea is not to show him up cause these backwoods rednecks ain't gonna appreciate nobody colored bein that full a himself. But if you show off what you can do and then let Jack and everybody else join in, folks'll go home feeling they got their money's worth."

"All right, Mister Rice."

"Okay. You go on in five minutes," he said and rushed off just as Diamond walked up.

"What do you think a the show?" Diamond asked.

"I don't know yet. I ain't used to white folks askin me what I think."

"Did you know who Daniel Bones was?"

"Not till he come off the stage and I saw him up close," Jim said.

"That Bones routine is somethin Rice just come up with."

"Here!" Rice said, putting something into Jim's hand and running off again. Jim looked in his hand and stared at the piece of burnt cork.

"What's wrong?" Diamond asked.

"What I need this for?"

"None of us really need it cept the people who pay to see us."

"What's wrong with seein me like I am?"

"We ain't in that business."

"I didn't know that what we do was any a my business," Jim said.

Diamond smiled, took the cork from Jim, struck a match and burned the end of the cork with the flame. He blew on it to cool it off and then smeared it on his own face.

"You know, my family came to this country from Ireland over twenty years ago. And the first lesson they taught me was that the sooner I forgot where I came from, the better off I was gonna be....My real name ain't Diamond. It's O'Rourke. Johnny O'Rourke. I changed it to Diamond after this guy saw me dance and said it was like lookin at a diamond in the mud. So I stuck with what made me like a diamond and scraped off what kept me in the mud. You got an advantage not many blacks get. You're a dancer on the top shelf. And there ain't no way whites can hate that out a you. And if you put this on, you can even beat them at their own skin game. Cause while they tryin like the devil to hate you for what you are, your face is makin em laugh at what you ain't."

"I don't think I like it too much havin my bones do one thing and my face do another," Jim said. "So I'm a leave my face the way it is."

"Suit yourself but it looks like you learning pretty quick how to tell white folks what you think," Diamond said, just as Rice walked on stage and started introducing the closing act.

"Tonight we gonna close the show with a Walkaround, matchin up one of the greatest jig dancers ever to heist his legs against a young up and comer who may be the next Master Juba! Ladies and Gents, get a good grab a yourselves cause you about to get your bones rattled! Here they are! Jack Diamond and Jim Crow!"

Jim and Diamond climbed up on the stage from opposite ends and stood facing each other about ten feet apart. The hum from people talking under their breath spread through the crowd. Diamond stretched his neck in Jim's direction and put his hand against his forehead, making it seem like he was looking at Jim from a long way off. Then Diamond started a slip-slide movement toward Jim but made no headway. People, who'd been upset by the sight of Jim, laughed at Diamond trying to cover a lot of ground and getting nowhere fast. Jim took that as his cue and started his own slip and slide away from Diamond without getting anywhere.

A second wave of laughter splashed through the audience and the last of the holdouts finally gave up. Not giving anybody a breather, Jim folded his arms and tapped on his toes and heels so fast nobody could see his feet leaving the floor. Diamond chased Jim's speedy steps with a swift-stepping jig of his own. The rush of their feet kept up and then slowed down before going back to chasing each other in a slip-slide that got them nowhere in a hurry.

The noise from the crowd reached up through the trees and into the heavens. The rest of the cast joined Jim and Diamond on stage to take their bows. Many people in the audience tried to get close enough to shake their hands and get a better look at them. Other folks kicked up some dancing dust of their own to prove they knew how to put on a show. Before long, everybody was so mixed together that you couldn't tell who was in the show from who had come to see it.

When Jim finally got back to the dressing area behind the bedsheets, he saw some white men talking to Rice. He couldn't hear what they were saying, but they didn't look like they'd had a good time.

"Jim," Diamond said, from behind him. "There's some people wanna talk to you."

42

He pointed into the darkness just past the string of bedsheets. Jim walked in the direction where Diamond had pointed and saw a group of blacks huddled together.

"You wanna see me?" he asked, when he'd gotten close enough. A woman stepped away from the others, and Jim was surprised by the cheekbones bulging like stones beneath her skin. She looked around to see if there was anyone near enough to hear them.

"We wanted to talk to you up close to make sure you was really the one we heard about."

The woman's eyes searched out something in Jim's face deeper than skin. "Whereabouts you from?" she asked.

"Around Louisville."

"So you the one whose dancin put so much giddy-up in colored folks, you had a be taken away 'fore everybody got rabbit in the blood?"

"How'd you hear bout it?"

"Our people pass the word more regular than we pass water!"

They all laughed but the woman got quiet again as though she was waiting for something.

"You still got people back where they took you from?" she asked.

Jim nodded.

"What name they go by?"

"My mama's name is Whisper. And my daddy's is Jim Crow, same as mine."

And then a thought hit him so hard his ears rang.

"You think you could find out where they at?"

"Ain't no tellin," she said. "We found out about you. So word could catch up with you in one a the towns you passin through."

"I'd be mighty grateful."

"We already grateful to you….But there's somethin else we wanna ask you."

She didn't move but Jim could feel something in her pulling the other people in closer.

"Can you read?" she asked, and then moved back like she wanted to give him more room to answer.

"No, I can't," Jim said, moving his eyes away from the woman for the first time. The woman looked at the people behind her and then turned back to Jim.

"That's all right," she said, touching his arm. "None a us can either. Ain't no shame in that. The shame is thinkin you ain't supposed to....You ought a think on it. Learnin to read, I mean. You could do it without puttin yourself in harm's way like we would, if we did it. And you never know. One day somebody like me might need you to read somethin that could help a lotta people out. If you get my meanin?"

"I understand," Jim said, and saw the woman staring at something behind him. He looked over his shoulder and saw Rice waving his hand to let him know he wanted to see him.

"We gonna get on our way now," she said, and squeezed both his hands in hers. This was done again by the others. And then they moved away and were swallowed up by the darkness.

Some of the actors were packing up all the things they used in the show and others were unwinding with bottles of whiskey and kegs of beer. Rice was seated in front of a looking glass, wiping off the last traces of make-up by the weak-burning flame of a lantern. Jim stood behind him and saw sadness in his eyes and in the corners of his mouth.

"Nothin's as good as when I'm performin," he said, more to himself than Jim. "And that's never more clear to me than when I look in the mirror after a show and wonder what I'm gonna do with myself until I get back on stage again."

He took a deep breath and remembered Jim was waiting behind him.

"What did those people want who you were talkin to?"

"They wanted to tell me how much they liked the show."

"You mean how much they liked YOU."

"It wasn't just me, Mister Rice. They liked everybody."

"You keep that act up and you'll do all right in this business....Well, I had some visitors too. But they wasn't that excited about you. Especially, since you didn't have on no black face."

"Wasn't my own face good enough?"

"They was wonderin whether you think you too good to put it on."

"It ain't that I think I'm too good for it, Mister Rice. It's just that I'm already colored."

"Forget about them for a second. What if I asked you to do it?"

"I can't do it, Mister Rice."

"You mean you won't....Suppose I told you, you had to do it or else you go back to Churchill?"

"That sounds like you in the same business as him."

"I'm just worried about some a these roughnecks bustin up the show or you, cause they think you tryin to be uppity. But maybe I'm makin somethin out a nothin?"

"Mister Rice, I wanna ask you somethin."

"What's that?"

"You heard anything from Mister Churchill bout my mama and daddy?"

"No!" he said, almost yelling. "I mean, as far as I know, they're all right....Look! If you don't wanna black up, then don't. But I wanna warn you that there're some places we perform where not puttin it on could be dangerous."

Jim didn't know what to make of Rice. Then he remembered what the woman said about learning to read. At the time, he'd only heard what she said. But after talking with Rice, he knew what she meant.

The next stop for Tom Rice's Non-Pareil Minstrel Show was in Lexington, Kentucky. Since they'd be in a good-sized city with a real theater, Rice told Jim that Lexington would be a better test for how well the show would do with a black dancer. On the train, Jim thought about how he could learn to read without anybody finding out. He decided to take a chance and told Jack Diamond about wanting to read. He tried not to make a big deal about it by saying if there were going to be stories written about him in the newspapers, he should at least be able to read them. He went on to say he'd never seen what his name looked like and wondered if Diamond would write it out for him. Diamond looked away and said he wasn't that good a speller but promised to find a way to help Jim if he could.

Jim had never been any place the size of Lexington. The road running through the center of town was packed with people on foot, horseback, and in horse-drawn buggies. Pigs, chickens, and cows bumped up against the two-legged creatures in the ankle-to-knee-deep mud. It seemed like everybody wanted to be seen. They strutted and opened their mouths wide, spitting out noises so fast that Jim couldn't understand any of it. But there was something about the way people threw their voices and bodies around that made him feel like he was watching a show right there in the muddy streets.

Jim decided to go to the theater early after Rice told him he couldn't stay at the hotel and would have to sleep in one of the dressing rooms. Rice tried to make him feel better by saying that over the years he'd slept in worse places than a theater. Jim stood at center stage and looked out over the large empty hall that stretched from the pit in front of the stage to the box seats stuck along the walls above, to the gallery way up high, almost touching the ceiling.

That night Jim watched from behind the curtain as people arrived. The pit was the first to fill up with folks who didn't seem sure of where their seats were. They were followed by a more well-to-do class of people in the box seats who knew exactly where they were supposed to be. The last group to come in poured into the gallery and didn't care where they sat. These were the cheapest seats and the only place where blacks were allowed.

Jim could also tell that people didn't act the same while they waited. Those in the box seats sat still; they only turned their heads to look at somebody or say something to the person next to them. In the gallery, women nursed babies while trying to keep older children quiet by poking them in the head with their knuckles. Other men and women ate and drank, throwing chicken bones into the aisles and spitting tobacco juice on the floor. The talk was loud and rowdy and a few fights broke out but ended after some punches, biting, and a few head butts. A woman in one of the boxes turned around to look up at the gallery while balancing a huge bowl of hair on her head.

"Why you lookin up here like you the colonel's lady?" a man yelled. "I bet your old lady was Rosie O'Grady!"

The theater shook from laughter as the woman snapped her head back around and turned up her nose.

"You got airs, do you? Well I got some airs for you," the man hollered. And he stood up, turned his backside to the woman and let go with a gust of gas that brought the house down in a tide of laughter.

It was only when the theater got dark that everybody finally quieted down. Jim went to his dressing room to do some knee bends. On his way back to watch the show from the wings offstage, he passed Diamond who walked by him and slipped something under his arm.

"What's this?" Jim asked, but Diamond had already gone to another part of the backstage area. It was a book. Jim looked around to see if anyone was watching him and then stuffed it into his back pocket. He got to his spot offstage in time to see Rice walk on stage. The gladhanding was mixed with cheers, whistles, and footstomping.

"First of all, I wanna know, how many of you out there AIN'T ladies or gentle men?"

Hissing and cursing came back at Rice as soon as the words were out of his mouth.

"All right!" he said, raising his arms for quiet. "That's good! Cause otherwise we'd have to sugar things up and you wouldn't get to see our real lowdown dirty dog of a show....But before we start, I wanna lay down the rules and regulations that the management has told me to tell you about: you can eat, whistle, and stomp your feet so nobody'll get it into their head that you don't know how to act. If you see somebody you know while the show's going on, give em a holler! If you see somebody you don't know, don't let that stop you from givin them a yell too. The spittoons you see all around are not for spittin but to pretty the place up a bit. So if you gotta spit, just let it fly! The most important thing is to have a good ole time. And if you didn't pay to get in, you probably enjoyin yourself already."

Rice went behind the curtains and the show started. The opening act had Rice as Mister Bones and another actor as Mister Tambo talking in fits and starts. They tied each other up into word knots and took the audience on a thought trail that was as mind-bending as the Lewis and Clark Expedition. Mister Tambo and Mister Bones ended their routine with Bones reaching into his baggy pants pocket, taking out a bar of soap, looking offstage, and getting water thrown on him. He then soaped up his wet hands and said to Mister Tambo: "I don't know bout you, but I'm washin my hands of this whole show!"

Bones tossed the soap to Tambo who did the same and they both left the stage. This was followed by four actors who did a scene from *Macbeth*. But the audience got restless and let them know about it when a man called out:

"Hey Macbeth! I got somethin for your bad breath!"

48

A rock whistled by the head of the actor playing Macbeth and the curtain closed to cheers that rocked the house.

At the intermission, Jim went back to his room. He opened the book and looked at the words and pictures on each page. After a few minutes, he figured out that the pictures told what the words looked like. He got so caught up in the book that he missed the start of the second half of the show.

When he got back to the wings, there was a skit going on about the travels of African Joe, a black-faced riverboat man in the mold of Mike Fink, who sang, danced, and fought his way up and down the Mississippi River. When it was over, the audience was on its feet and African Joe swaggered offstage, bragging on himself:

"My mammy was a wolf. My daddy was a tiger. I'm what you call an old Virginia nigra. Half fire, half smoke. A little touch of thunder. I'm what they call the eighth wonder!"

But the audience that couldn't get enough of African Joe didn't find Jim and Jack Diamond all that tasty. Grumbling started and got louder as Jim and Diamond told more of their heel and toe story. Jim never saw the rock but heard it ricochet off the stage and bounce through the curtains.

"You walkin too good!" a man yelled from the gallery.

"You in the wrong place with the wrong face!" another man hollered, just as a second rock wheezed by Jim's ear.

"You either gonna give us some black face or WE gonna give you a bloody one!"

Jim and Diamond didn't stop but they kept their eyes on the gallery.

"Where you get that WE shit?" someone yelled from the gallery.

"The same place I always gets it! With my foot up your ass!"

The two men rushed at each other, and the crash of their heads knocked them both out cold. Fights broke out all over the gallery. Rice waved Jim and Diamond off the stage as he and the other actors came out and took their places.

With bone clappers, tambourines, and banjos, Rice and several cast members copied the slugfest going on in the gallery until their clowning got to be a better show than the fighting. And when those who were fighting couldn't hold anybody's attention except the one they were hitting, they gave up and turned back to the stage.

Once the audience was back where he wanted them, Rice and the other actors fell out on the floor like they were pooped out.

"Is there a doctor in the house?" Rice said. "If not, then somebody ought a fetch one quick. None of our shows ever ended like this. But that just shows to go you that the Non-Pareil Minstrel Show packs a wallop. So come back again and tell your friends. I know some a you may not a liked seein a colored boy in the show. But maybe that's cause you just ain't use to it yet. But I betcha, the more you see Jim Crow, the more you gonna feel like you wanna see him again. Mark my words!"

After the audience had filed out of the theater, Rice went to Jim's dressing room.

"You know, you're right," he said. "It's better if you don't put on no burnt cork. I should a built you up more. That way, people would a been more prepared for what they got. Folks get spooked when they get more than what they expect. I'll do better next time."

"I ain't sure if your better and my better is the same," Jim said.

"As long as we both get what we want, I don't think they'll be no problem."

"What you want might cost me my life, Mister Rice."

"What I want ain't half as dangerous as the freedom you think you want."

"Nothing scares me bout freedom cept somebody trying to keep me from it."

"Sometimes that's the same person tryin to get it."

A smile creased Jim's mouth.

"Well, if the day ever come when I'm my own worst enemy, least I'll know who I can count on for help."

"While you waitin for that to happen, let's go over to the hotel," Rice said.

"What for?"

"Some people at the show tonight are throwin a little shindig for us."

"I thought I wasn't allowed in there."

"It's just for tonight. Everybody from the high and mighty to the low and humble wanna get a better look at you."

Jim walked into the saloon of the hotel with Rice and Diamond. All at once, they were swallowed up in the same crowd who'd come to see the show. But this time, they were all thrown together with nothing in the way except their bodies. The people who'd been sitting in the best seats had on masks and were bumping and rubbing up against folks they never got within smelling distance of—at least not when they were out in public. Blacks and whites whose place in the scheme of things was near or at the bottom dressed up in fancy clothes and put on the airs of folks who lived in the big house. Actors in the show were surrounded by people wanting to have their faces blackened. Once they were smeared up, they acted out scenes from the show and even made up some of their own.

It was no surprise that Jim got the most attention. Some people just stared. Others came up and touched him as if they wanted to find out what he was made of. And a few just stood close to him and breathed in his smell like they were trying to take what was inside him into themselves.

"He don't look like he can do all the stuff he was doin."

"How's somebody supposed to look who can do what he can?"

"Who you keepin company with inside you?" a white woman asked.

"Just myself, Mam," Jim said, looking right at her.

"Watch it boy!" a man said. "Don't let me catch you wrong by lookin too long."

"No Suh!" Jim said, jerking his eyes away.

"With what you can do with those legs a yours, I bet you got a powerful drumstick!"

"No Suh!" Jim said, getting scared he was going to say the wrong thing.

"Oh leave the boy alone! Can't you see you scaring him?"

"You see his skin? Look like it been scraped right off the bark of a cinnamon tree."

"I guess we know what other color been keepin company inside him."

"So what! Ain't that what this whole shindig's about? Getting close to things we ain't supposed to be near!"

"But he ain't made up like the rest! Boy! How come you ain't blacked up like everybody else in the show?"

"Suh, I can't do what the white folks do, only what they say do!"

"I like that! I like that!"

It took some doing but Jim finally got away from the crush of eyes, hands, and questions. He stumbled out into the street and through his watery eyes saw men and women throwing things on the ground. Some of them got into carriages and others made their way out of town, walking like they were more than a little tipsy. Jim rubbed his eyes and when they cleared, he saw wigs, hairpieces, underclothes, and outerclothes on the ground that had been worn by people at the party.

Jim walked back to the theater and went in through the rear door. As he passed the dressing room down the hall from his, the door opened. A well-dressed white man stood in the doorway. The surprise on the man's face was the same as Jim's when he looked past the man to see Tom Rice, naked to the waist. Rice nodded and the man rushed past Jim and through the back door of the theater.

Jim didn't know what to do and was angry that Rice didn't seem upset.

"You wanna see me about somethin, Jim?"

"No!" Jim said, almost shouting.

"Well, I'm a finish dressing and go back over to the hotel. I'll see you tomorrow."

He closed the door and left Jim steaming in his own breath.

After seeing people who couldn't stand Jim and others who couldn't get enough of him, Rice tried to find ways to get folks to see the show no matter how they felt. He decided to send an actor to whatever town or city they were supposed to be in next. When he got there, he spread the word about this colored dancer with magic in his feet. By the time he left, people were chomping at the bit to see Jim Crow.

On the train to Paducah, Jim kept pretty much to himself and studied the words in the speller. Even though the other actors didn't ignore him as much as before, Rice told the cast that the success of the show was riding on making Jim bigger-than-life. So it was better for the show if he was left alone and had the Jim Crow car all to himself.

When the train pulled slowly into Paducah, people were lined up in front of the station four and five deep. Hunched backs straightened up through spines and necks to get a better look at this black man who they'd heard kicked up such a fuss with his feet. Jim waited until everybody else left the train before getting off. He came down the steps, and when his feet touched the ground, he felt the pebble-filled dirt push against the soles of his shoes. Jim moved his feet back and forth, making a cloud of dust that came up to his knees. He then led the rest of the Tom Rice Non-Pareil Minstrel Show into the center of town with the crowd following the trail of dirt.

The company was put up at a boardinghouse, and a place was found for Jim in a barn. In the afternoon before the opening night of the show, the cast did a run-through. During a break, Diamond came over to Jim.

"Where'd you get that dust step you did yesterday?"

"It come to me when I was gettin off the train."

"No tellin what you'd a done if you had more time to think about it."

"If I'd a thought about it too much, I wouldn't a done nothin."

"You been keepin pretty much to yourself lately."

"Ain't that for the good a the show?"

"Yeah, I know all that. But I get the feelin there's somethin else up with you."

"Well, there is, sort of," Jim said.

"What is it?"

"Somethin happened when I went back to my room after that shindig in Lexington."

"Yeah?"

"Rice was in one of the dressing rooms."

"He does that a lot. He can't stand to leave a theater sometimes. He'll sleep there, even if he's got a hotel room."

"He wasn't alone!"

"So?"

"It was a man!"

"That bother you?" Diamond asked.

"It don't bother you?"

"You know, I'll never forget the day those two bounty hunters brung you into Louisville tied across that horse like a sack a flour....THAT bothered me!"

Jim stared at Diamond and felt the same as he did when he saw that man coming out of the dressing room with Rice standing half-naked inside.

Something poked Jim in his sleep. He woke up to the smell of vinegar and someone standing over him. It was a woman with sweat shining on her face like brass. She was wearing a one-piece sleeveless shift and was rubbing her right hand up and down her left arm.

"Who you?" Jim asked.

"I'm the one who might be lookin for you," she said, wiping

her forehead with the back of her hand.

"Why?"

"Anyone ever ask you if you understand mouth on paper?"

"Once."

"What'd you say?"

"No."

"What you say now?"

"Yeah."

The woman turned away, took something from inside her clothes and faced him again. She handed Jim a piece of paper that was crumpled up.

"What this say?" she said.

"Wait a minute! You ain't told me nothin about you yet."

"I'm from round here," she said. "Name's Bernadine."

"Where'd you hear bout me?" Jim asked.

"Word a mouth. Now, can you gimme the mouth on the top a that paper?"

Jim opened it up and stared at the printed words.

"It say, North Star."

"That's enough for right now."

"What you mean?"

"There's more than just me you need to read it to."

"Where they at?"

"After the show tonight, I'll take you to em."

"What's North Star?" Jim asked.

"It's a mouth paper put out by a colored man named Frederick Douglass."

"Who's Frederick Douglass?"

"You can find out tonight right along with the rest of us."

Bernadine stopped rubbing her arm and stared at Jim like there was something in him she was looking for.

"There's somethin I gotta tell you," she said.

"What!"

"It's about your daddy....He was lynched near about a year ago....He beat his massa to death with his own cane. Even after all the life was choked out a him, they say his legs kept jumpin like he was dancin on air. Nobody would touch him. The white folks couldn't get none a the colored to cut him down till his legs stopped movin."

Jim didn't want her to stop talking. But when she did, the quiet in his head and mouth was filled up with the words that gave back to him the hurt he'd given his father. I DON'T WANT NO NAME THAT SOUNDS LIKE I'M THE SAME AS YOU!

"What about my mama?" he asked, forcing the words out of his mouth.

"All a the massa's slaves been sold off. And there ain't no word on where she at....I wish there was something I could tell you that'd be a comfort. But there ain't."

She moved closer and put her hand on his shoulder. When she was gone, he still felt the weight of her hand and Whisper's words—EVERY GOODBYE AIN'T GONE. But how could that be, he thought, if HELLO wasn't nowhere to be found.

Before the show that night, Jim found Rice in his dressing room picking through rag-tail pieces of clothes that he wore in his act. They hadn't said too much to each other since that night and usually stayed out of each other's way.

"Mister Rice."

"Oh, Jim! After that ruckus you kicked up at the train station, it looks like all of Paducah's gonna be here tonight!"

"Did you know my daddy was lynched?"

"How did you …"

It was too late. And there was nowhere to hide from the words that had come out of his mouth.

"Who told you?"

"Who told me don't matter as much as YOU not tellin me!"

"I was goin to....It was just a matter of findin the right time."

"You mean in YOUR own good time, don't you, Mister Rice?"

"All right. I should a told you. But if I'd a done it before, you'd a probably run off half-cocked without realizin what you got goin for yourself in this show."

"Yeah. I know what I got goin for myself. It's the same thing you got goin for you. ME!"

"At least with the show, there's somethin in it for you," Rice said. "There ain't nothin for you in slavery."

Jim went to his dressing room and didn't come out until show time. He didn't watch from the wings that night but stood in the back alley where he heard the crowd noise coming from inside. When the time came for Jim to go on, he went in and heard the last of the word play between Mister Tambo and Mister Bones. The news about Jim's father had gotten around, and the rest of the actors were waiting to see what he was going to do.

"Here's the moment I know you all been waitin for," Rice said. "We call em our two-legged high-steppers: Jack Diamond and Jim Crow! So here's hopin you get lost in their shuffle."

Jim watched from offstage as Diamond started. He was looking at him but not really paying attention. Then he saw something in Diamond's step that he hadn't seen before. It wasn't just a lighter touch in his footwork but a lot more action in his arms and shoulders. Diamond had taken some of what he was doing from Jim. But there were other moves and sounds coming off the bottoms of his boots that were all his own. And at the moment when Jim felt himself sinking from somebody dumping rocks in his soul, Jack Diamond pulled him out of the lowdown hole he was in.

Jim came on stage while the audience was still giving Diamond a hefty-sized helping of hand clapping. He didn't wait for quiet but stood in the middle of the stage and jerked his head left and right. The jerking got hold of his arms and legs, making him loose-limbed. Then his legs started getting a life of their own. He turned his knees in, toe-stomped one foot and then the other into the floor, jumped straight up, and came down rocking back on his heels before realizing he was doing the first dance his father ever taught him. Hadn't he told Jim to take whatever was useful from what he gave him and let the rest go? So he kept serving up the best parts of his father to the audience and then did something he'd never done before when he was dancing. He spoke out loud:

Wheel about
turn about
do just so
and every time I wheel about
I jump Jim Crow

The crowd was on its feet, sweating and screaming for more. But Jim slipped off the stage doing a walking dead dance that sunk him back down in the rock-load of sorrow weighing on his mind.

The woman called Bernadine was waiting for Jim when he got to the barn. She didn't speak but started walking. So he followed. Jim didn't know where he was, and in the pitch dark night, he followed her by the sound of her bare feet on the ground.

"Wait," she said, stopping.

"What is it?" he said. "You hear somethin?"

"Come on," she said.

They walked on, and the smell of horse manure was everywhere. Soon Jim was able to make out what he thought was a shack. Bernardine opened the door and he followed her in. They stood in the dark until a candle was lit. In the flickering candlelight, there were ten or more black people sitting on the floor. They didn't look at Jim but were eying the flame dancing on the candle wick. Bernadine pointed to a place on the floor for Jim to sit down.

"Whenever you ready," she said.

Jim pulled the paper out of his pocket and someone passed him the candle so he could see. He stared at the page, his mind doing battle with all the words jammed up together.

"This man Douglass is saying that the *North Star* is in favor of colored people bein free. He say this paper gonna shout out loud for our rights but just as loud about our faults. It ain't gonna give no rest to slavery in the South, and hold no t-r-u-c-e with our op-pres-sors in the North....E-ve-ry ef-fort to in-jure or de-grade you or your cause shall find in the *North Star* a con-stant, un-swer-ving and in-flex-i-ble foe....We shall e-ner-ge-ti-cal-ly as-sail the ram-parts of sla-ve-ry and pre-ju-dice be they com-posed of church or state, and seek the de-struc-tion of e-ve-ry re-fuge of lies, under which ty-ran-ny may aim to con-ceal and pro-tect it-self."

Jim looked up and their eyes were on him like fish on bait.

"He somethin ain't he?" Bernadine said.

"How long he been in freedom?" a man asked.

"Near bout ten years," another said.

"And he ain't the only one," Bernadine put in. "More 'n more colored is lightin out for the Promised Land every day. And there's many more like Douglass helpin em get there."

"Well he sure know his way around them words," a woman said.

"You told the gospel on that," another said.

"I never heard of him 'fore today," Jim said.

"That's why we need what you got there in your hand," Bernadine said, "and more folks like you who can read what's on it."

"We much obliged to you, Crow, for comin out here," a man said.

"I'm the one should be doin the thankin. I got a lot more from you than you got by havin me read this."

"Word a mouth and mouth on paper is both hearsay," a man said. "One's no better than the other. What's better is knowin both."

"Speakin a hearsay," another man said, "we heard tell about the ruckus your dancin kicked up in Louisville. I didn't believe it till I saw what you did to folks tonight. With Douglass settin our minds on fire when he gets his jaws to goin and your feet puttin the rabbit in our blood every time we get too set in our ways, there ain't no way we can lose!"

They all laughed, forgetting that making too much noise could let the wrong people know what they were up to.

"You gotta look out for yourself," Bernadine said. "There's plenty whites don't like it when they see you actin like you full a yourself and not them....You need to be gettin back."

After shaking hands all around, Jim followed Bernadine back into the pitch black night.

"You live anywhere near where we just come from?" Jim asked.

"Not far. Why?"

"I was wonderin if you got family?"

"If you mean blood kin, no."

"Where they at?"

"I never knew my mama or my daddy. I was raised by different people till I was eleven. I did whatever else I needed to make myself grown after that. The only thing I know bout my mama was that she led a slave uprisin back in '22 while she was carryin me. She was taken with some others. And right after she birthed me, she was lynched."

Jim couldn't see Bernadine's face, but her words hung in the air.

"You got children?"

"No."

"How come?"

"Never saw no point in it. Havin what you can't keep. So I don't put nothin in my life that I can't do without."

"You got a man?"

"When I want one."

They didn't say anything else, and the only sounds they made came from moving through the thick underbrush pressing in on their bodies. When they got to the place where the features of the barn could be seen, Bernadine stopped.

"I'm a leave you here," she said.

Jim didn't move or speak.

"What is it?" she asked.

"It ain't what. It's you," he said.

"What about me?"

"That's what I wanna find out."

"Well. You gonna show me the way or do I gotta do that too?"

Lying on their sides, Bernadine watched Jim stare at their shadows made by the flame in the lantern. She moved closer, making the straw underneath them sound like fire chewing through kindling.

"You been with anybody before?" she asked.

He shook his head without looking at her. She pulled him to her and slowly traced her fingers along the bone bridge between his shoulders and then fingered every one of his joints at the neck, shoulders, elbows, wrists, fingers, hips, knees, ankles, and toes. When she was sure he was all there, she helped him take off his clothes and then had him help her. She pulled his hands to her and took him wherever her skin was hungry. And when he found all the places she was waiting to feel, she gave him her pleasure—not just there or there but everywhere!

Jim and Bernadine were asleep on the straw when they woke up to men all around them with blackened faces and the color of milk around the mouth. The men grabbed them, stood them up and put knives to their throats.

"We was wonderin if you was ever gonna show up, nigger! But it looks like our wait paid off just like yours."

Bernadine didn't move an inch. Her eyes seemed like they were looking at something far away.

"We ain't done nothin," Jim said.

"It ain't what you done. It's what you didn't do," said one of the milk-mouth faces.

"Yeah," another said. "We wanna see darkies when we go to a

62

show, not some uppity nigger who think he too good to act the coon like he supposed to!"

"Look at my face," a milk-mouth said. "This how you supposed to look!"

A hand smeared cork on Jim's cheeks and forehead.

"That's better," the mouth said. "Now all we gotta do is make it so you keep a grin on your face!"

Bernadine screamed just before the blade jerked the corner of Jim's mouth and ripped open his cheek. He cried out as the knife set fire to his face.

Then voices stabbed the air with Jim's name and large fireflies swarmed into the barn. The men in black faces left Jim and Bernadine to meet the fireflies and the voices that were moving closer and shouting, "Jim! Where are you? You all right?" But the voices turned into more black-faced men holding fireflies that were really lanterns. One group of black faces stared at the other group without moving or saying a word until a voice broke the spell.

"We're over here! Jim's hurt!" Bernadine shouted while pressing a balled-up piece of her dress against Jim's face. The black faces and milk-white mouths went at each other. And in the tumble and tussle that followed, no one was sure of who was who. So they tried wiping the black off the face of whoever they were fighting with, but not letting anyone do it to them. This took the fight out of everybody. And it was all the black-faced, milk-white mouths who hurt Jim could do to high-tail it out of there before they got too tired to get away.

When Tom Rice, Jack Diamond, and some of the other actors finally got to Jim and Bernadine, there was blood everywhere but they both were covering their mouths to keep what sounded like laughter from coming out.

"You two gone loony or somethin?" Rice said.

"If you could a seen yourselves. I never thought I'd live to see the day white folks'd be trying so hard to keep some other white folks from findin out that they both white," Jim said, grinning through a face covered with cork, blood, and tears.

Rice, Diamond, and the others looked at one another and then at Jim and Bernadine who were doing all they could to cry to keep from laughing.

It wasn't long before Tom Rice was thinking about ways to put what happened in Paducah into the show. But while Rice was thinking up new gimmicks to get people's attention, the government was putting on a show to settle the argument over slavery that had the whole country riled up. Blacks didn't like the idea that even though slavery was at centerstage of all the talk about the future of the country, the government only wanted to set a limit on the states where it could be taken on the road. But blacks didn't let that stop them from walking out on slavery wherever it was playing.

Tom Rice's Non-Pareil Minstrel Show played to full houses wherever it went. And Jim had gotten even more popular after Paducah. All the attention bothered him because he knew people wanted to look at his face for the same reasons they came to see the other actors in black face. Everybody else could wipe their faces off at the end of the show. But like his color, the scar, growing like a worm out of the corner of his mouth, was there for good. Jim became very moody and didn't talk to anyone except Jack Diamond. He even stopped acting in skits with the other actors so he wouldn't have to be around them. Many in the show started saying among themselves that Jim had gotten as good at playing the dandy as Rice was at playing the darky.

While Rice didn't like the change in Jim, he had other things on his mind. He was still working on his skit about the attack on Jim in Paducah. But he decided not to tell anyone until it was finished. When the skit was done, Rice told everyone else before he talked with Jim. Things between them had gotten worse after Jim found out that Rice had known about his father being lynched.

On a train to Cincinnati, Rice walked into the Jim Crow car and was surprised to find Jim reading a newspaper.

"I didn't know you could read," he said.

"You know how it is, Mister Rice? Being Jim Crow means I gotta keep a lotta things to myself."

"I got a new skit I wanna run by you. I got the idea from when those rednecks cut you in Paducah. The way it goes is—we'd all be in black face on one side of our face and white on the other. When we start talkin out of both sides of our faces, you try to figure out who's on your side and who ain't. We keep the audience guessin right along with you until the end when everybody finds out who's who."

Jim tried not to laugh, but couldn't help himself and felt the usual itch in his scarred cheek.

Rice smiled.

"I was hopin you'd like it," he said.

"No you wasn't, Mister Rice. You was hopin I'd be in it. But like I told you before, I wanna do what I do by myself."

Rice shook his head.

"I'm not askin you to black up."

"I still ain't gon'do it."

"I guess what everybody's been sayin bout you is true?"

"What's that?"

"That you done turned into a duded-up slave actin like some white-assed dandy!"

"I had me some good teachers."

"Jim, don't you think you carryin this act a yours a little too far?"

"Ain't that what bein a minstrel's all about?"

"You know what I'm talkin about."

"Yeah. I know. You think I don't buck in the middle enough. Well, this took all the buck out a me!" Jim said, pointing to his scar.

"I ain't sayin you have to wipe your face on nobody's ass. But you gotta understand that if you wasn't in this show and acted the way you act, you wouldn't be scarred for life. You'd be dead! One way or another, you gonna have to accept that, slave or free, white folks and maybe even some a your own people ain't gonna 'low you to act like you dance when you come offstage....Even I got sense enough to know that the life I got once I come off-stage ain't never gonna be more than an intermission between shows."

"Inna-mission? Is that what you call what you was doin when that man come out your dressing room?" Jim said, snapping the newspaper open in front of his face so he wouldn't have to look at Rice.

Rice smiled, turned to leave the car but stopped.

"I know you ain't had much practice yet. But lemme know what it does for you to feel like you better than me."

Rice's new skit opened in Cincinnati and was called, "WHO'S WHO IN PADUCAH?" Jim didn't change his mind about not wanting to be in it. Another actor was picked for the lead role of a fugitive slave who got into town just ahead of slave-catchers and hid in a theater while a minstrel show was going on. The slave-catchers spotted the slave slipping in the back door of the theater. They followed him inside; and when they saw all the actors onstage in black face, they blackened their own faces so the escaped slave wouldn't notice them. They found him back-stage and chased him through the curtains into the middle of a scene full of actors in black face. The black-faced actors, the escaped black-faced slave, and the black-faced slave-catchers got so tangled together that everyone had a hold of something that belonged to someone else. The skit ended when the black-faced slave got lost in the mix-up of black-faced white actors and slave-catchers with none of them knowing who anyone was. The the-ater rocked from the side-splitting laughter of the audience, and the cast closed out the show singing the title song, "Who's Who In Paducah?"

Tom Rice's Non-Pareil Minstrel Show played to standing-room-only crowds for the whole five-day run in Cincinnati. It was a hit in cities and towns all along the Ohio River and made Tom Rice the most famous minstrel in the country. "WHO'S WHO IN PADUCAH?" became the most loved popular entertainment in America until a book came on the scene that shook the nation up, first on the page and then on the stage. It was called *UNCLE TOM'S CABIN!*

When Jim danced alone on stage in Cincinnati, people didn't get as mean as they'd been in other places. This might've had something to do with "Who's Who In Paducah?" which put a tickle in the skin and a laugh in every bone. And by the time Jim came on, no one got too worked up over watching a black man who did everything with his body they wanted him to do except bow and scrape. On the last night of their run, Diamond stuck his head into Jim's dressing room after the show.

"There's someone here to see you," he said, and left before Jim could ask who it was. The door was partly open, but no one came in.

"Come on, if you comin!" Jim said.

The door swung all the way open and a man the color of brand-new copper stood in the doorway. His unbuttoned waistcoat gave way to a vest that blossomed into a fluffy shirt and a head of curly hair held down by a hat shaped like an overturned flower pot. The man's legs swelled inside his pants, looking like they were the offspring of a tree trunk.

"I'm William Lane," he said.

Jim couldn't believe it! He was in the same room with the great Master Juba—the man many said was the greatest dancer that ever was and the first black dancer to get top billing in an all-white minstrel show.

"Come in," Jim said, getting up and putting his hand out. "Mister Lane. I was hopin' I'd meet you one day. Please, sit down."

Lane sat down, crossed his legs, took off his hat, and held it in his lap.

"I came to find out if what they say about you is true."

"What's that?" Jim asked.

"That you the best thing to hit the ground on two feet since me....After seein you tonight, I knew we'd met before. Not face to face. But in another way that counts for more."

"So what you think?" Jim asked, not wanting to pass up the chance to be praised by the great Master Juba.

"If you need me to tell you what you already know, then I guess we both wrong about you."

The words stung and Jim tried to change the subject.

"You ever go up against Jack Diamond?"

"Jack Diamond's the best jigger that ever was. I never out-danced him. I just outlasted him."

Lane stared across the room like he was remembering some-thing.

"But that time's long gone....There's a fuse burning in this country and it's connected to slavery. And I don't wanna be here when it blows."

"Where you gonna go?"

"I been invited to England. The money's better than anything I'd make if I stayed here. And if I had any doubts about leavin, seein you dance convinced me that I made the right decision."

"What did I do?"

"It ain't what you did. It's how you went about doin it. You didn't show me nothin dancewise that I didn't expect to see. What I wasn't sure about was somethin else that burned inside a me when I was your age. I knew you had it the moment I saw you. It made me feel good, but I was sorry too cause it's a bless-ing and a curse."

"I don't understand."

"There's a power in you that's got nothin to do with wanting it. A lot of our people have it. But when you live in a country where people got so much hate in them, you can find yourself turning away from the power inside you and wanting the power others have over you. I don't want that to happen to me. But if I stay here, it will."

"You sayin, I wanna be like the ones that done this to me?"

70

Jim said, pointing at his scar.

"I'm sayin, sometimes you can lose your way."

"You ever been in slavery, Mister Lane?"

"No."

"Maybe if you was, you'd know it ain't so easy talkin about losin your way when you ain't never had your own way to begin with."

Lane got up from his chair, put his hat on his head, patted the top with the palm of his hand, and reached out to shake Jim's hand.

"I'll tell you what," Lane said. "I know I'm right about me. But if I come back, you can tell me if you was right about you."

Wherever Jim traveled, he met secretly with blacks and read them newspaper stories about the full-blown storm kicking up over slavery. He also carried messages about slaves who were traveling on the Underground Railroad. But in all his travels, there was never any news about Whisper. Whenever the show played in Paducah, Jim would look up Bernadine, hoping she had heard something.

After years of moving in and around the mid-section of the country, Jim knew the strange and twisting ways that made one city different from another. He could tell even the smallest change in the way people acted around each other. On this trip to Paducah, Jim saw more upset in the faces of blacks than he'd ever seen before.

On a charcoal-dark night, Jim made his way to Bernadine's cabin, using his memory to guide him. When he was almost there, he felt someone near him.

"Jim?"

" 'Nadine?"

"There's a meetin inside," she said, pressing her body against him. There were more people than usual. Bernadine handed him the *North Star*.

"We already know what it say," a man said.

Jim read to himself. The highest court in the land had handed down a decision about a black man named Dred Scott who, while traveling with his master in free territory, lit out for freedom on the grounds that he was in a territory that was free according to something called the Missouri Compromise. But the Court didn't hear it his way and said that the white men who set up the country never meant for blacks to be citizens. So they didn't have any rights under the law ...

Jim looked up after he'd finished.

"From what that paper say," a man said, "there ain't no way to freedom in this land. Wherever we go, we end up back where we come from!"

"So what if that's what IT means!" Bernadine said. "It ain't sayin nothin we don't already know. The thing we need to study on is what WE mean to do!"

"Don't you understand, woman! It don't matter worth a damn what anybody colored got in mind to do cause the law ain't takin us into account!"

"I don't know bout nobody else. But I ain't plannin to stay put," Bernadine said. "I'm goin where I ain't never been!"

Much later, Jim and Bernadine lay in a corner of the room, holding onto their thoughts as tightly as they held each other.

"Why you jump on Malachi like that?" Jim asked.

"He scared me. It's like he given up. I don't know what's got into him. But I don't wanna catch it!"

"From what I been seein, somethin's caught hold a colored folks but it don't look like what bit Malachi."

"Jim ... I'm leavin here," Bernadine whispered.

"Where to?"

"Freedom."

"Then what?"

"Come back and help others do the same."

"How'm I gonna see you?"

"You can come with me."

Jim figured Bernadine would say that. But he didn't expect to feel what finally came out of his mouth.

"I don't think I can do that."

"Why not?"

"It'd mean I'd have to let the dancin go."

"No it wouldn't. You'd just have to let Rice go."

"The slave-catchers would be on me quicker than soon."

"No quicker than they'd be on anybody else. But that ain't what's botherin you? Is it?"

"Look, 'Nadine … I gotta dance in front a people. But if I run off, I won't be able to do that no more."

"Why you gotta have a lot a people around? You wanna be free or you wanna be seen?"

"For me to be free, I gotta be seen. I can't hide out."

"So you think you got it better under slavery than you'd have it bein free?"

"No. I'm just better off when I'm free to dance the way I wanna."

"I'm glad for you Jim cause, like I told you when we first met, I ain't never had nothin a my own that I thought I could keep, includin my own life. You truly blessed. And I curse the day I ever laid eyes on you!"

She sucked in a breath of air and squeezed him tighter.

"Course, I can't say the same for my hands."

"How long before you leavin?" Jim asked.

"Could be anytime. I'm just waitin for word."

"Can I help?"

"Just hold me and don't talk. But I want you gone when I wake up. That way I won't have to remember seein you leave."

There was no spite in Bernadine's voice, but each word moved her further and further away from him. As she slept, Jim felt her breath on his arm. Right before dawn, he dressed and looked at her one last time. She was hunched under a blanket with her head resting on her hands which were pressed together. It was like she was listening to herself sleep to find out something she would need to know when she woke up.

Jim was surprised that Bernadine had slept so well their last night together. His decision not to go with her seemed to rest a lot easier with her than it did with him. He was bothered by what she'd said about him wanting to dance in Rice's minstrel show instead of being on his own. Had the Jim Crow car and all that went into making Jim the man with the flying feet become who he was? Was bein "a big to-do" more important to him now than dancing or even taking his freedom? Maybe that's what William Lane was trying to tell him? That at some point, without knowing it, he wanted dancing to bring him more than just the joy of doing it. But Jim wasn't sure if the man they called "Master Juba" left the country because dancing was no longer enough in a country about to leap, headlong, into a civil war.

Tom Rice heard all the let's-giddy-up-and-go-to-war talk just like everybody else; and he decided to put shows together that played both ends of the talk about slavery and freedom against something funny in the middle. Whites were coming into theaters with anger stewing in their bellies, and it didn't take much to put them in a fighting mood. By the time Jim came on stage, looking like he was about to burst from being so full of himself, white folks, without a pot to piss in, were ready to take a swing at somebody. But since the government wasn't around, they hauled off on each other or whoever happened to be on stage at the time.

All the actors in the show were having problems drawing the line for people in the audience between what was make-believe and what was real. The line was being crossed everywhere they played and Rice did what he could to take the steam out of any skit that might get folks too hot and bothered. During a swing through towns along the Ohio and Kentucky borders in the early spring of 1861, Rice came into the Jim Crow car in black face.

"It's a little early for that, ain't it?" Jim said.

"I dunno, Jim. Here of late, I been thinkin maybe I should wear this all the time except during the show....I wanna talk to you about a few things. The first has to do with the car."

"What car?"

"This one. You riding all by yourself like this don't help the show the way it used to. Instead a makin folks come to the show hungry, they comin ugly. Course, it really ain't the car. It's the country. We at the end and the beginnin of somethin. And I don't know how to play to it anymore."

Jim rubbed his scar.

"I catch your drift, Mister Rice. Sometimes this car does feel more like a coffin than a coach. I guess the way things are now, it's better if we all travel Jim Crow style."

They both laughed and in the quiet that followed, Rice seemed to be listening to himself think.

"You know, I been meanin to say somethin to you about that night I saw you outside my dressing room."

Jim's back tightened up.

"When you looked at me, it was like I was seein somebody I hadn't seen in a long time but couldn't place the face. Later I knew why I couldn't remember the look on your face. I'd never seen it on nobody colored before. More than likely that's cause I ain't never paid that much attention. I've seen it on white faces all my life. My own included. Maybe that's part a the reason why I put on this burnt cork. It's a way for me to fight that look on my own face and the feelin behind it. I didn't wanna admit that it hurt when you looked at me. But it did. That's why I didn't tell you about your father....I keep thinkin—maybe if I'd talked to you about how that look made me feel, I might not of hurt you back. But I guess when you come down to it, there ain't much chance, the way the country is now, of folks doin much of anything that don't hurt somebody."

Jim felt like he was floating inside himself and losing the battle to keep above the surface of everything he thought he knew.

"I don't know what to say, Mister Rice," he said.

"Don't you think it's time you stopped callin me Mister Rice?"

"I guess that means there was a time when you felt it was all right for me to call you that?" Jim said, smiling.

"It didn't take you long to find somethin to say," Rice said. "You know, we'd make a great Mister Tambo and Mister Bones. I'd set you up with the lines and you could come back at me like you just did. You been doin it offstage for years. Might as well bring it into the show, so everybody else can see it."

"I'll do it. But we gotta wear our own faces."

"I don't know if I'm ready for that," Rice said.

"Me neither."

"But what about the Mister business? You ready for that?"

"I was born ready for that!"

"Well, when you gonna start?"

"Don't worry. You'll be the first to hear."

"There's somethin else I wanna get squared away with you," Rice said.

"What's that?"

"After Churchill died, everybody was sold off to a man named Jameson. He's the one who got the papers on you. I been payin him to keep you in the show. But if somethin happens to me, I don't know what he's liable to do. I only met him once, so I don't really have a good read on him. Course, if I was you, the only thing I'd need to know is—he owns slaves. So he must want em cause, otherwise, why does he have em? All I'm sayin is: this country's about to blow up in our faces and I thought you ought to know the man's name."

"Thanks, Rice."

The train made a water stop, and all the members of the show crowded into the Jim Crow car for the first time. The talk was loose and tasty with more mischief than they'd had together offstage in years. Jim sat next to Jack Diamond, thinking about his talk earlier with Rice.

"Maybe we ought a do the show right in here," Jim said.

"Why not? We the best audience we've had in some time....So what you think about havin to share your car with the rest of us low-life air-breathers!"

"I like it fine. Like I told Rice, I'm tired a carryin your butts. It's time you started totin your own weight."

"You mean to tell me that all this time it wasn't your ass you had on your shoulders, but ours?"

Jim laughed so hard his scar started to itch.

"You ever known Rice to leave the black on his face like that?" Jim asked.

"Not this long."

"What do you mean?"

"He's afraid," Diamond said.

"Of what?"

"Same thing everybody's afraid of. Havin what you're used to pulled out from under you. Rice needs to be on a stage in black face. Cause if he ain't, he don't have no idea who he is or what he's doin. Which puts him several cuts above most men I've known who do a lotta damage tryin too hard to be white."

Jim and Diamond agreed to do the Walk Around to end the show that night, something they hadn't done together in years. They swapped steps and added a new twist at the end of each one for the other to play with. But the audience got restless when the battle of steps didn't seem to be building to a point where Diamond would come out on top.

"Come on!" a man yelled. "We had enough a the howdy. Now let's get rowdy!"

"Yeah!" someone else shouted. "Come on you fuckin mick! Jig that nigger off the stage!"

There was more yelling and cursing as Jim and Diamond started getting worried. Rice walked on stage and waved at them to come off. He was hit with boos as he tried to get the audience to quiet down.

"Hey! What you tryin to do? Steal our blunder? We the ones supposed to provide the insult and injury in this show. Not you."

Laughter watered down some of the anger and Rice tried to take advantage of it.

"We're here to act the fool, make fun, and run with all our might, but without a fight."

"Well, we wanna fuckin fight!" a man shouted.

"You gotta make up your mind," Rice said. "Which one do you wanna do?"

"That's right, minstrel man. That's what you good at. Ridin the fence. But you can't have your ass on both sides no more!"

"I don't take sides up here," Rice said. "I take bows!"

The laughter moved the crowd in Rice's favor again and he bowed.

"You trying to make a fool out a me?" the man shouted.

"Sir. If you come in here with two hind legs, you don't give me much choice."

The laughter cooled off the heat of the moment. The man kept on shouting, but he was drowned out. Rice laughed along with the audience and bowed again as cheering rang out from the rafters. He looked offstage and signaled the rest of the cast to join him for a final bow.

Rice was unbelievable, Jim thought, as he came back on stage with the others. Diamond was right. This was where Rice was at his best. He would never be as good anywhere as he was on stage. Jim looked down the line at the other actors, and Rice caught his eye just before his black face was twisted into a sick frown by the sight of a man in front of the stage. He shouted something at Rice, raised his arm to point, turned and ran up the center aisle. Rice clapped his hand over his mouth. And his chest started heaving like he was laughing at something the man had said. Then he stumbled backwards the way he always did in his drunk routine. But when he took his hand away, screams greeted the blood that shot out of his mouth.

When Tom Rice was shot in the mouth, his body bucked like a horse before he died. The man who killed him was chased into a blacksmith's shop where he shot himself in the head rather than give himself up. Before taking his own life, he shouted out his loyalty to the Confederacy, and said he shot Rice to sound the call to battle like the one heard two days earlier on April 12, 1861, when Fort Sumter was fired on.

Rice was laid out on a table in a dressing room. A towel was put over his face to hide the horrible gunshot wound. Jim, Diamond, and the rest of the company were standing around the table when the doctor arrived. He examined the wound but seemed more upset by the black-faced actors watching him than the mess that was left of Rice's face. When he finished, he washed his hands in a basin of water but had problems getting all of the burnt cork off.

"What's this stuff made of?" he asked.

"It's somethin the deceased came up with," Jack said. "Chicken bone marrow and horse piss!"

The doctor looked at Diamond and let him know he didn't think that was funny. He wiped his hands on a towel, closed his bag, and left the room, slamming the door behind him. Everyone held onto their poker faces. And when they couldn't hold them anymore, they started spitting up laughter.

Most of the cast agreed to take Rice's body back to New York City for burial. Jim wasn't sure about what to do because a part of him wanted to go back to Louisville to look for Whisper. But Diamond told him it wasn't a good idea to try to find his mother with the country going to war with itself.

They all got on the train in western Kentucky and traveled in a car whose windows were covered with the colors of mourning. All along the train route, people who'd once turned out to see Tom Rice's Non-Pareil Minstrel Show were lined up along the tracks. And as the very young to the very old tried to hold that moment when the funeral car passed, Jim watched from a window as the size of people and towns got smaller, and along with them the hope of him ever finding Whisper.

The train moved east through Ohio and Pennsylvania. At a stop in Lewistown, Pennsylvania, Jim took a walk and saw a crowd made up of blacks who were listening to a black man speak. He spoke with his whole body, using his arms like a swimmer to get his words to where they were going.

"The time of deliverance is at hand," he said, putting his hands out in front of him with the palms up. "But there's all kinds a hands. And we need all the hands we can get, 'specially the ones at the end of our wrists. So let's never forget to give ourselves a hand at the same time we accept a hand from somebody else."

The man grabbed his left hand with his right.

"What's in my hand?" he shouted.

"Your hand!" the crowd yelled.

"What's in your hand?" he shouted back.

"My hand!" the crowd yelled, as each person held up one hand in the other.

"Whose hand?" the man said.

"Mine!"

"Whose hand?"

"Mine!"

The man moved into the crowd, grabbing hold of one hand after another. When he grabbed Jim's hand, he held it a little longer as he looked at him.

Jim walked back to the train station thinking about that black man who had spoken his mind in public.

"You get a good look at the town?" Diamond asked, when Jim got back to the station.

"I not only got a eyeful but a earful too."

"You there!" a voice called out.

Jim turned around and saw the black man who'd made the speech. There were some men, women, and children around him. Jim poked his finger into his chest and the man nodded. He excused himself from Diamond and walked over to them. The man was standing still, but the spitfire from what he'd said before was in his eyes.

"You the one they call Jim Crow?"

Jim nodded.

"You come in on the funeral car?"

"Yeah."

"I'm Rayfield Wilson," the man said, sticking his hand out. "I've heard a lot about you."

"Well, I don't know what you heard. But listening to you a while ago was the first time I've seen a colored man talk out loud and not worry bout who heard him."

"People tell me that's what you been doin for years."

"It's good a you to say that but I don't think my dancin's anywhere near as loud and clear as what you got to say."

"Look at this boy's face?" Wilson, said, putting his arm around a boy's shoulders.

Jim looked down at the boy who stared at him wide-eyed.

"You know who this is?" Wilson asked the boy.

"He's Jim Crow!"

"How'd you hear bout him?"

"From my daddy."

"What he tell you?"

"That his dancin make people wanna jump up and get free."

"Now this boy ain't never laid eyes on you. But thanks to his daddy, what you've done is in his mind. And he ain't the only one. There're others here who seen you dance before or heard about you. If I talk till kingdom come, I'm never gonna see the look this boy give you!"

"I oughta be gettin back," Jim said, starting to feel uncomfortable.

"Whose body's on that train?" Wilson asked.

"Thomas Rice."

"Who was he?"

"He's the one who ran the show I was in."

"Well, if he's dead, the show's over. Ain't it?"

"Yeah, but some of us from the show is takin him back to New York for burial."

"You gonna follow him into the ground too."

"It was good meetin you, Mister Wilson," Jim said, putting his hand out. But instead of shaking his hand, Wilson grabbed Jim's arm.

"You got any idea of the power you have?" he said, squeezing it.

"Let go my arm!"

Wilson let go.

"It's a shame," he said. "I only had your arm. But it seem like that dead white man got a lot more of a hold on you than that."

Wilson grinned with a lot of devilment in it. It reminded Jim of Rice when he played Mister Bones. He and another actor who was playing Mister Tambo would be slugging it out with words. And there was always a moment when Rice would come back at Mister Tambo with something he'd thought up right on the spot. The pleasure he took from that had as much to do with the words he used as it did with the truth of what he said. It didn't matter if what Wilson said was true. Jim could tell Wilson was lit up with satisfaction. He'd turned the table of words on him, and, in the bargain, won over everybody who was listening.

Jim got on the train and turned to see Rayfield Wilson working another crowd up into a lather. Wilson was standing on a keg. He lifted his head up a bit and caught sight of Jim who, before going into the car, nodded in defeat for having been bested by another Mister Bones.

The train pulled into New York City, and steam gushed from underneath the engine. It mixed with the thick smoke coughing from factories and made it impossible for Jim to see the sky. The river-wide streets were choked with people, horses, and carriages. No one seemed to be able to keep still and Jim was worn out just from watching.

Rice's body was taken in a hearse to a hall near the lower tip of Manhattan known as the Five Points district—whose name came from five streets meeting at a place called Paradise Square. Jim, Jack Diamond, and the other actors found a place to stay on a street lined with whorehouses and saloons. The water from sewers was backed up into the street and back-alley privies were flooded.

None of this surprised Jim. But his mouth dropped open when he found out that blacks and whites lived in the same houses. He listened to the sounds coming from open windows and how the fast-moving and song-like voices from black and Irish folks made a kind of music out of all the rough and foul talk.

That evening Diamond took Jim to one of the local saloons. Diamond was spotted as soon as they walked in, and a group of men and women came over to the bar to welcome them.

"It true like they say that Tommy took a shot in the mouth?" a woman asked.

Diamond nodded. "Just when we was takin our bows at the end of the show."

"Tommy always knew how to close a show," the woman said, with pride. "It's a real tribute to him that he stirred up that man's passion so much that he was moved to take Tommy's life instead a askin for his money back."

84

"I'll drink to that!" a man said.

"Oh shut up, McVie!" the woman said. "You'd drink to anything if it meant you could drink up everything!"

Everyone at the bar busted out in laughter.

"I'm surprised Tommy didn't spit that bullet right back in the face of that Secesh," the bartender said. "I watched him throw stiffer shots of whiskey down his throat than any powder that could a been in that bullet!"

"Well, Shaughnessy. If gun powder is stronger than whiskey," a man said, "I wish you'd start putting it in the liquor, 'stead a waterin it down like you do."

When the laughing simmered down, no one spoke for a while.

"This here's Jim Crow," Diamond said. "The dancer you all heard about."

"I hear you as good as Master Juba," a woman said.

"Naw. I ain't even as good as I can get."

"You keep talkin like that, you just might make somethin out a yourself!"

Word had gotten around that Tommy Rice had come home. And they came from every direction leading to the Five Points district. People packed into the saloon called The Jig. The crowd was larger than what was allowed under the city's fire regulations, but firemen from the local station house stood at the door in case any fire inspectors showed up.

The coffin holding Rice's body was on a platform, and the members of his Non-Pareil Minstrel Show stood behind it. A priest walked up to the lip of the stage, faced the crowd, and took off his collar.

"As devoted as Tommy was to blasphemy, I won't embarrass him by making this a sacred occasion. But while Tommy was blasphemous, he was never cruel or disrespectful. He hid behind disguises so we could see ourselves through his effort to find himself. And if we came away not feeling as good about what made us laugh, the more we thought about it, we were all the better for it. I've always believed Tommy and I were doing the same kind of work. You come to see me about things that are no laughing matter. And when you went to see him, he made you laugh at the same things you talked to me about in private....Fate has now seen fit to take this holy fool away from us at the moment when his disguises could show us the folly of dressing ourselves in blue and gray....This is no laughing matter. But if Tommy were here, he would show us that if we can only save the Union by killing each other, no one will get the last laugh."

The priest put his collar back on and left the front of the stage to a respectful helping of applause.

Jack Diamond stepped in front of the coffin and raised his hands for quiet.

"We wanna try to keep things movin along cause we know Tommy wouldn't a wanted the bar shut down for too long on his account. Plus, the Department of Health told us we gotta get Tommy in the ground tonight. We got him iced up so he won't get too ripe on us....So let's get on with our respects to Tommy. Everybody was given a piece a cork when they came in. So any of you that are of a mind to, I'd like you to do this."

Diamond took a piece of burnt cork out of his pocket and put a streak of black across his forehead and both cheeks. Jim watched as blacks and whites all over the saloon blacked-up their faces. Diamond offered his cork to Jim but he shook his head. Diamond opened his mouth to say something but stopped himself before turning to face the crowd again.

"We'd like you to join us now in singin Tommy's most famous song: 'Who's Who In Paducah?' "

Are we who we are when we open our eyes?
Is my face myself or just a disguise?
Do we know who's who when our eyes are shut?
When the lids go down, do we know what's what?

In a place called Paducah, a Negro was cut.
And when his rescuers met his attackers,
They was both blacked up.
In the muscle and tussle their faces was smeared,

Till no one knew who was to be feared,
But they all knew with their eyes open wide,
They were better off not knowing
Who was on the other side.

So this is the story of how faces can fool yuh.
How it's best not to know,
Who's who in Paducah.

Diamond turned to Jim. "Before we put Tommy underneath the ground he had such a good time on top of, I'm gonna ask Jim Crow to have his say."

Jim walked to the coffin, leaned over, put his head against the side, and started beating on the top with his hands. The rhythm of his hands against the wood was picked up by his feet. He then climbed on the coffin, and stood up on top of it; and while keeping his balance, he stamped down a jig that put a thump in the heart and a lump in the throat of everyone who could hear his feet.

After Tom Rice's funeral, most of the actors in his Non-Pareil Minstrel Show left New York for places unknown. Jim and Jack Diamond stayed and made a little money in contests pitting them against other dancers. But once folks got wind of the fact that anybody going up against them was overmatched, all bets were off. The only contest people were willing to wager on was one between the two of them. But Jim and Diamond had agreed not to be a part of any contest against each other.

When Jim wasn't looking for work, he would go to the saloons and dives along the streets of the Five Points district. It was there that he met black men and women whose dreams to form their own minstrel shows had been stalled by the war. They all got together at The Jig, ran their mouths, and worked out dance routines on a thick butcher block. Two of the people Jim got to know were Jubilee and Zulema. When talking to either one of them, no one could ignore Jubilee's fleshy lips around his large mouth and Zulema's thick-fingered hands that shaped her thoughts in the air when she spoke.

"Nowadays, havin the gift of song and dance ain't enough," Jubilee said. "You gotta have a gimmick."

"I heard that!" Zulema said, nodding her head. "Unless I'm a payin customer, the only way for me to get in one a these shows is by playin the part of a man!"

"Didn't 'Honest' Abe say somethin about not bein able to fool people but for so long?" Jim asked.

"I only wanna fool some a the people, part a the time," Jubilee said.

"And what do you do the rest of the time?"

"I cut the fool without gettin paid!"

Jim shook his head and laughed along with Zulema.

"I been meanin to ask you somethin," Jubilee said, looking over at Jim. "How come you didn't put on no black-up like the rest of us at Tom Rice's funeral?"

"I don't use it!"

"Not even for Rice?"

"Not for nobody!"

"Good thing for you, your face ain't your bread and butter," Zulema said.

"What I don't understand," Jim said, "is why anybody colored would start blackin-up now after all the years of seeing white folks doin it?"

"When I black-up," Jubilee said, "I ain't gotta follow in behind what no white man did who put it on before me. Which ain't gon be the case for all these colored men rushin to put on that Yankee blue!"

"You tryin to tell me there's less shame for a colored man puttin on burnt cork than joinin the Union Army?" Jim asked.

"All I'm sayin is—everybody got their reasons for what they do. The way I see it, black face ain't no different from a uniform. And I can say the same thing all these Negroes runnin round wantin to be soldiers are sayin: havin somethin on me don't mean it gotta be in me!"

"If more colored women thought that way about you men," Zulema said, "we'd be a lot better off."

"There you go again! Low-ratin the colored man!"

"Jubilee? Why is it, when you have your say, you just speakin your mind? But when I speak mine, I'm tearin the colored man down?"

"Why you gotta have so much to say all the time?"

"Cause I got a lot in me that needs to get said! What's wrong? Afraid there won't be nothin left for you to say?"

"There's always gonna be somethin left for me to say."

"Then what you worried about?"

"Nothin!" Jubilee said, picking up two cups from the bar, opening his mouth into a yawn, and putting a cup in the wide open space of each cheek. He then removed the cups, leaned back against the bar and folded his arms as everyone in The Jig stared at him with their jaws dropped.

"Nobody can say I got that from no white minstrel," he said.

"That ain't somethin I'd wanna brag about," Jim said.

"Why not? Loadin up my mouth like that is what people gonna remember me for long after they forget your dancin."

"I'm glad you gonna be remembered for havin your mouth fulla something other than what you usually got in it," Zulema said.

"What you got to offer that's any better?"

"Since we womenfolk offered up every one of you men into this life, I think anything else we do gotta be better than that!"

"You sound like you don't care much for the male part a the human race?"

"Oh, I guess you all mean well. It's just that when you get to doin what you got in mind, you pitiful."

"You puttin Mister Jim Crow in any a that?"

"Whatever you tryin to start, I ain't in it," Zulema said.

"Me neither," Jim said.

"Right," Jubilee said softly and moved closer to Jim. "You ain't never been in nothin cept that fancy Jim Crow car. But all that's over now."

He picked a pear out of a bowl of fruit on the bar.

"This war's gonna bust this country wide open," he said, squeezing the pear, crushing it, then putting it slowly into his mouth and chewing it. "And I'm gonna eat as much of it as I can stand. And if there's any left, you and Zulema can have it. You understand me?" he said, poking his tubby finger into Jim's chest.

Jim knocked his hand away.

"Be careful," he said, feeling the muscles in the back of his neck tense up.

Jubilee's head snapped back and he let out a sick-sounding laugh.

"You don't know how careful I'm bein. You and them white

90

folks you think I'm tryin to please better hope I never stop laughin!"

He spit out a piece of the pear on the floor at Jim's feet and walked out of The Jig. His laughter could still be heard inside long after he'd closed the door behind him.

Jim found out that Jubilee wasn't the only one who needed to laugh at things that were no laughing matter. At every saloon he went to in the Five Points district, laughter was laced with anger when stories were told about top-of-the-heap politicians in the North who were behind the illegal sale of weapons to the Confederacy in exchange for Texas cotton that would be sold to New England mills. There was also a knee-slapping story about a popular new concentrated lemonade that was making a mint for the William Morris Company, who advertised it as the best friend in the Union soldier arsenal during any attack of scurvy.

The regulars at bars laughed until their throats were raw. But when they swallowed, the raspy taste in their throats turned to a cough, reminding them that the nation's family squabble had gone on longer than anyone had figured it would. The war was ending up taking the most from those who never had very much to begin with. And Jim saw it in people walking the streets all the time: their faces slammed shut against anybody trying to get anymore from them.

While all this was going on offstage, Jubilee was causing quite a ruckus onstage. Being able to put just about anything in his mouth got the attention of the Christy Minstrels, who hired him for their Broadway show. In one skit, a black-faced white man of considerable means and schemes pulled the wool over Jubilee's eyes by holding his coat in front of Jubilee's corked face while tricking him out of his pocket watch. By winter time, the man had pulled every stitch of clothing he had on over Jubilee's eyes and wasn't wearing anything except his long underwear. The black-faced white man shivered in the cold but instead of taking back the wool covering Jubilee's eyes to warm himself, he froze to death. In the end, Jubilee's mouth and mind were still as gullible as ever, but the white man who took advantage of him outsmarted himself because he valued his pride more than his own life.

Jubilee's nightly performance made the Christy Minstrels the most popular minstrel company in New York, and he became the best-known black entertainer in the city. But as Jubilee's star rose, Jim had to make do with dancing in saloons. There was still interest in his squaring off with Jack Diamond, but only if there were a clear winner and loser.

One night Diamond came into one of the dives where Jim danced. During a break, Jim joined Diamond at the bar.

"Since when you come in here?" Jim asked.

"Every now and again, I like to take a look at a good hoofer workin his trade."

"Who you shittin?"

"Everything's changed, Jim. Minstrelsy has up and left us bustin our own dust."

"What you gettin at?"

"The other night I saw a cockfight. That's what people wanna see. Two humans heeled up with spurs like roosters, goin at it till one or both of em give out."

"That sound like war to me."

"You think what we do in these dives for pocket change is dancin?"

"Not so far as I can tell."

"So. What's the difference? Let's give em what they want."

"What they want is for you to cut me down to size!"

"So what! You know what size you cut as a man. Whatever happens is over when the contest ends."

"You know better, Jack. The war got everybody's blood up. I can feel it even down here in the Five Points."

"You think you too good for me to get the better of you, don't you?"

"Shit, Jack! You know that ain't it."

"I should tell you somethin you need to know. There's talk

that if you don't go along, your walkin days is over."

"Jack! I didn't know you was workin for Western Union."

"Jim, this ain't no idle threat."

"Well you can tell em for me ..."

"Jim," Diamond said, grabbing his arm, "listen to me. The men I'm talkin bout are out a work Irish riffraff with a lotta time on their hands. A lot's been taken from em and they wanna even the score by goin after what keeps you alive. So if you don't entertain em in one way, they'll find another."

Jim lay in bed that night and smelled the fear in his sweat. He touched his cheek, tracing his finger along the scar that inspired Tom Rice's famous song: "Who's Who In Paducah?" What had scared him the most was wondering what those white men were going to do and almost being glad when they finally cut him. He shuddered at the thought of going through that again. Then his sweat chilled to ice water and he knew what he was going to do.

Jubilee burst through the doors of The Jig, fresh from his nightly performance on Broadway. He was slapped on the back and crowded into a corner by people wanting to be in his company and hoping to catch some of his good fortune. After a few rounds of drinks and much glad-handing, Jubilee looked around The Jig for some other familiar faces. He spotted Jim at the other end of the bar.

"Well, if it ain't Mister Big Stuff! I hear you gonna be goin heel and toe with Jack Diamond this Friday."

Jim said nothing.

"What's the matter? Your mouth in jail or something?"

Jim turned his head slowly in Jubilee's direction.

"I don't wanna talk about it."

"Yeah! And I bet you don't wanna dance neither. But you goin to. Ain't you? I wonder what got you to change your mind?"

Jubilee walked over and stood next to Jim.

"Maybe they promised to cut you another smile up to the other ear!"

"Get out of my face, Jubilee!"

"I'm in your face!" Jubilee said, moving so close their heads almost touched.

Jim shoved the heel of his hand into Jubilee's mouth. Jubilee touched his bleeding bottom lip with his fingers and sucked the blood from the bruise.

"Oh! Yes! Yes!" Jubilee hissed, and then bent his head and charged Jim.

Shaughnessy, the bartender, was over the bar quickly, holding a three-foot-long club.

"You two gonna have to take that out a here," he said.

"Far as I'm concerned, you ain't gonna chew that but once,"

Jubilee said.

"Don't fight him!" Zulema pleaded, grabbing Jim's arm. "Look at him, Jim! This ain't got nothin to do with what just happened! It's about somethin he had set in his mind about you long before he ever laid eyes on you!"

Jim was gasping for breath, having had the wind knocked out of him when Jubilee's head rammed into his stomach.

"It don't matter to me when we do it," Jubilee said. "But it ain't gonna be over till we settle it. So I'll either see you now or I'll see you later."

He walked past Jim toward the rear of the saloon and through a door. Fear banged in Jim's chest, sucking all the strength out of him. Zulema was right, he thought. But it was too late to do anything other than what Jubilee wanted. Jim started toward the back door, and his legs dragged like they were filled with sand.

The whole saloon emptied out into the alley behind Jim. Lanterns were hung from hooks, and the crowd boxed them in by forming a circle along the sides of other buildings.

"Now you gonna feel what it's like to have me in your face!" Jubilee said, rushing at Jim, who tried to hold him off but wasn't strong enough. Jubilee held Jim with one arm and drove his other ham-sized fist into Jim's arms, thighs, and ribs. Every blow, whether it landed solidly or glanced off Jim's squirming body, hurt like a toothache. Just when Jim felt he couldn't take another punch, his body started to feel numb.

Egged on by the crowd, Jubilee felt the same excitement he had in front of an audience that was enjoying a show.

"I'm glad it's gettin as good to you as it is to me!" Jubilee said to the crowd.

He let Jim fall to the ground and stood over him.

"Now that I've cut you down a few pegs, I'm a make you a face like mine."

Jubilee grabbed a handful of Jim's shirt collar and lifted him up.

"First the lips," he said and tilted his head back and butted

96

him in the mouth.

Jim's head snapped back and his legs collapsed under him. He looked up at Jubilee standing over him. The shouts from the crowd seemed far away.

Jubilee knelt down.

"Now I'm a give your mouth some more size."

Jim twisted his head away as Jubilee tried to pry open his mouth.

"Guess I'm a have to knock you out first," he said, raising his fist.

Glass shattered!

Jubilee reacted to the sound, jumped to his feet, and grabbed his right arm which was stinging. Zulema stood a few feet away, holding only the handle and jagged mouth of a beer mug. The crowd was quiet but eager to see what would happen next.

"What's matter with you, 'lema?" Jubilee said, pressing his left hand over the nasty gash in his right forearm. "You really think I was gonna hurt him that bad?"

"I didn't think! I knew!"

"So what now?"

"It's over."

"For who?"

"For everybody."

"If you don't like the show, then leave."

"You the one gonna leave."

"Why don't you put that down?" Jubilee said, making a move toward her.

"Come on! And I'll shove this so far down your mouth you won't be able to talk without cuttin your fuckin throat!"

Jubilee studied Zulema and decided her fury was wound up too tight for him to chance another move toward her. He could also feel that the giddy mood of the crowd and his own heady excitement had fizzled out.

"Well, you fucked up the fun, 'lema. I hope this don't become no habit. Cause if it do, you better know what you doin....Ask your friend here. He knows what I'm talkin bout."

Jubilee moved toward the closed circle of people. A space opened up for him to pass through. But just before heading out of the alley to the street, he looked back at Zulema standing near Jim with the handle of the broken beer mug still in her hand.

"You know, 'lema. In this life, laughin at somethin terrible is sometimes the difference between livin and dyin."

Zulema helped Jim back to his room, tore a bedsheet into strips, wrapped them around his bruised ribs, and sponged away the blood that was caked into his split lips. Jim watched her with the same attention she gave his injuries. Zulema's hair was pulled back tightly, which lengthened the smooth mocha slope of her forehead into her scalp. She sniffed back tears, and Jim admired the magnificent spread of her nose, almost equal in width to her mouth.

"I 'preciate what you did out there," Jim said.

"I don't know what I would a done if Jubilee had come at me."

"That's why he backed off. He didn't wanna find out."

Zulema helped Jim onto his bed and then collapsed into a chair.

"There's somethin I don't understand," she said.

"What's that?"

"I was watchin your face when he was hittin you. And it was like you didn't care."

"Not hardly! It's just that when he kept hittin me in the same spot, I didn't have to worry bout what he was gonna do next."

"Yeah! Until he did somethin different."

"Right!"

"What was all that crazy talk Jubilee was doin about people laughin to keep from dyin?" Zulema asked.

"That's why he's so good on stage. He can make people laugh at what they afraid of. And he's better at it than anybody I ever seen."

"I didn't see you laughin."

"He wasn't tryin to make me laugh."

"You make it sound like what he was doin to you was the same as puttin on a show."

"To him it was. Everything's all mixed up together. It used to be that *Uncle Tom's Cabin* was the number one show. Now, the biggest show goin is The War."

"So where does that leave you?"

"Dancin on butcher blocks in saloons. What about you?"

"That's a question I'm gonna answer one a these days. But in the meantime, I'll keep imitatin men."

"What you mean?"

"Just what I said. Men play the few women parts that turn up in minstrel shows. So I end up playin men."

"Where?"

"I been playin Mister Tambo, Mister Bones, and everything in between ever since I come to New York."

"Where you from?"

"Maryland. My daddy bought his freedom, my mama's and mine, when I wasn't much more than snatch away from after-birth. We come to New York about 1840. There was always music around. Both my mama and my daddy could make just about anything they touched sing. So whatever gift I got, I come by it through them."

"Well, when you play Mister Tambo and Mister Bones, you do em both at the same time?"

"White men in black face the only ones think they can be two people at once."

"And what you think you doin when you decked out like a man?"

"But I ain't a man."

"White men ain't black neither."

"It ain't the same thing."

"Why not?"

"What I do on stage ain't what I wanna do. It's what I gotta do, if I wanna be on stage at all."

"It was the same for me with dancin," Jim said.

"No it wasn't. Dancin's always been YOU. Men ain't never been ME."

100

"What are you, then?"

"I'm some a what I see, a lotta what I can't see, and hardly nothin of what you men see."

On the night of the contest with Jack Diamond, Jim remembered what Zulema had said. He knew his dancing set him apart from just about everybody. It had been men, sometimes black but mostly white, who used his dancing to make him pay for being different. But unlike Zulema, he at least paid the price for who he was and not for who he wasn't.

The crowds started arriving about nightfall at the waterfront, near the tip of Manhattan. A platform had been built about the same size as those used to stage boxing matches. Arm wrestling and head butting were going on to pass the time before the main event. Those who weren't interested in throwing their bodies around threw words around instead. Making his way to the platform, Jim heard the talk as it broke off into pieces.

"In war, there's always some that have to die so the many can live!"

"No! You got it backwards! In war, it's the many that have to die, so the few who started it don't have to!"

"Them's fightin words!"

"Yours are dyin words!"

Jim passed some soldiers who stared at him and smiled at one another. Right after passing them, he heard their voices shouting at his back.

"To the flag we are pledged./ All foes we abhor./ And we ain't for the nigger./ But we are for the war."

Jim slowed up as they laughed but kept on walking. When he got to the stage, there was a man already on it, holding a rolled-up rug and trying to get his attention. It was only when the man lifted the floppy hat covering his face and pulled off the fake mustache that Jim realized it was Zulema! She then put her disguise back into place and rolled out the rug to the edge of the stage where a black man grabbed both ends that had dropped over the side.

"I'm a tell you a story," she said, facing the audience and standing on a portion of the rug. "It's about a man trying to make his way but everywhere he turns the world is ..."

Before Zulema could say another word, the man holding the rug yanked it. She scrambled to keep from falling and the crowd fell out laughing every time the story called for the world to be pulled out from under her. But with each character she played who was down on his luck and attacked by villains that people hissed every time she twisted her handlebar mustache, there weren't as many laughs in the audience as before. And by the time Zulema took her final fall, the truth underneath what was funny about how she fell could only hold enough laughs to fill a cup.

When it was time for Jim and Jack Diamond to go on, the mood of the crowd had turned ugly. They started screaming for Jim's blood while they were both still limbering up.

"How you like being back?" Jack said, pointing to the crowd.

"I like it fine. They've done everythin cept kill me."

"Least the public's givin you somethin to look forward to."

"White folks always wanna give me what I don't need."

"Ready?" Jack asked.

"Ready or not!"

"Who first?"

Jim pointed at Diamond who started slowly by lifting one leg and bringing it down just before raising the other. He quickened his step and within seconds his legs were moving faster than anybody's eyes could keep up with.

The cheers from the crowd shook the stage and made Jim feel like his back was buzzing. He started out with high leg lifts and followed by turning his toes and knees in and out. The crowd held its breath. Then shouts against him and in his favor set fireworks off in the air.

"Go head, Crow! You the Mister Do Good of dance!"

102

"Better sit on them hands if you know what's good for you!"

"I'm doin what's GOOD for me!"

"It won't be GOOD for long, once I DO somethin to you!"

"Why don't you take all that mean mouthin you doin on away from here!"

"I find the mouth that go with them words, your face and ass gon be in the same place!"

"If you can do all that, you ought a join the Union Army. The war be over by next week!"

"I ain't fightin to give no nigger the right to take my livin away from me!"

"You keep messin with me, you won't have to worry bout makin a livin. Cause I'm a take yuh fuckin life!"

In another part of the crowd, people started singing and it spread quickly, drowning out all fussing with words.

"I wish I was in the land of cotton/cinnamon seed and sandy bottom/Look away, look away, look away, Dixieland/Then I wish I was in Dixie/Hooray, Hooray/In Dixie's land we took our stand to live and die in Dixie/Away, away …"

"You better put a hush up on that Reb song! That's treason!"

"Away down south in Dixie …"

"That ain't no Reb song."

"What's Dixie then, if it ain't the South?"

"It's a song about a darkie named Dixie!"

"Then hoe it down and scratch your gravel/To Dixie's land I'm bound to travel/Look away, look away, look away Dixie land…."

"What the Secesh look like singin a song 'bout some nigger?"

"They wanna live and die in the land of cotton just like the darky in the song."

"Ain't no white man, Reb or Blue Belly, gonna be followin in behind nothin no zip coon wanna do!"

"It was a white man from the North what wrote the song."

"Dixie land where I was born in/Early on one frosty mornin/Look away! Look away! Look away! Dixie Land."

"Who was that?"

"Dancin Danny Emmett!"

"How come you know so much? You some kinda spy for the Rebs?"

"Why I gotta be a spy just cause I know more'n you?"

"Who says you know more'n me?"

"You do, every time you open your fuckin mouth!"

The words gave way to pushing and shoving, which gave way to punches, kicks, sticks, bottles, and clubs. And the long-awaited contest between Jim Crow and Jack Diamond became a sideshow as the police moved in to break up the fighting and send the crowd home.

Like every other section of the city, those living in the Five Points district roused themselves on December 31, 1862, to find some reason to celebrate the beginning of a new year. Jim, Zulema, and Diamond were at The Jig waiting for 1863 to show itself. Afterwards, Jim and Jack would dance at a few local saloons until dawn. The hands on the clock face above the bar were fifteen minutes shy of midnight. The door opened, and Jubilee came in.

"Long as you got Jubilee, you ain't gotta worry bout Robert E. Lee," he said loudly.

Jim hadn't spoken to Jubilee since the night in the alley and didn't turn around. Jubilee walked over to the bar and stood next to Diamond.

"I'd go easy on that Robert E. Lee stuff if I was you, Jubilee," Shaughnessy said, leaning over the bar. "There's more'n a few in here that think they got more to fear from you than Lee."

Jubilee turned around and leaned back against the bar.

"Shaughnessy! A round on me for everybody!"

Some stayed put out of pride. Others were already too drunk to move. The few who finally dragged themselves to the bar ordered their drinks but didn't give up any thank yous.

Diamond turned toward Jim and Zulema, who still hadn't

looked in Jubilee's direction. He shrugged and ordered a double whiskey. Jubilee let his eyes roam the saloon with his usual skin-stretching grin and didn't seem bothered that no one was bending themselves all out of shape to be in his company.

While Jubilee made a big show of his success and others at The Jig nursed their bad luck and troubles with drink, the telegraph keys at Western Union offices in Washington began to click. At the stroke of midnight, the message was received by key operators all over New York City. No sooner did folks ring in the New Year than men from telegraph offices ran out coatless into the cold, yelling as the breath rushed from their mouths carrying the news. Stacks of tied newspapers with bold print on the front page were thrown from horse-drawn wagons. Boys grabbed all they could carry and hawked them in the streets.

A black man ran into The Jig out of breath.

"You hear what Lincoln done gone and did?" he shouted, only stopping to take a breath. "He done gave the order freein colored folks in every state that ain't loyal to the Union."

The man turned and was out the door. Just about everyone turned to look at the person closest to them but without saying anything. Jubilee slapped his thigh and let out a low rumbling laugh.

"Well, ain't that somethin! Lincoln finally givin us what we been takin for years without his permission. So now, when you hear the word Jubilee, people won't just be talkin bout me."

"What you think gonna come a this?" Jim asked Zulema.

"A lot!" she said. "For better and worse."

"What you mean by worse?"

"Lincoln didn't come up with this 'mancipation all by himself. The whole country studyin on what this freedom gonna mean. Most of us lookin forward to it. But there's whites and even some of us that afraid of it."

"Maybe now, some of us'll get to join in and do some fightin," Jim said.

"You wanna fight for the Union Army?" Diamond asked.

"Not for the Union Army. For myself!"

"You put the man's uniform on, you fight for what he want you to fight for," Jubilee said.

"Like you said: puttin on the uniform's the same as puttin on the mask," Jim said, grinding anger between his teeth.

"Listen to you! You against blackin up but you ready to do white face in the Union Army. Ain't you somethin! Shaughnessy! Another round for everybody!"

Jubilee slapped the money down on the bar, pushed himself away from it, and headed for the door. Everyone had another drink on Jubilee and huddled up in their own thoughts. This was not the case in the streets outside The Jig as voices were heard rising up in a mist of song:

Slavery chain done broke at last!
Broke at last! Broke at last!
Slavery chain done broke at last!
Gonna praise God till I die!

That spring Jim heard that Frederick Douglass was going to speak in Philadelphia. He decided to go, not only to see the great man, but to hear Douglass's reasons for wanting blacks to fight for the Union. At the train station on the morning Jim was leaving, the conductor pointed to him.

"First car behind the engine," he said.

Jim turned around just before boarding the train but didn't see the conductor telling anyone else which car to ride in. The car was about half-filled with blacks. Jim took a seat next to a man and watched blacks continue to file into the car.

"You travel by train much?" he asked the man.

"Now and again," the man said.

"I was just wonderin cause it seem like all the colored folks ridin in this car."

106

"So?"

"It's just that the conductor told me to ride in this car, but he didn't say anything to the white folks behind me."

"Ain't you been on a train before?"

"Plenty times."

"Then you either funnin with me or you crazy as a jaybird."

"You sayin, we ain't allowed in the same car with white folks?"

"Well now!" the man said, smiling. "I'm glad you back from wherever you been hidin yourself!"

At the station in Philadelphia, Jim was given directions to the church where Douglass was speaking. The church was on a narrow street of frame houses that were crammed together. It was the last house on the block and seemed to be leaning off to one side.

Jim took a seat in the back of the packed church and had to strain to get a better look at the speakers seated in the front. Even from that distance, he could tell which one was Douglass from the eyes that went right through you and the thick, woolly hair rising high above his forehead. When Douglass was finally introduced, he stood up, and his body spread out from his vest-covered chest, up the sleeves of his coat, to his bull neck and out of his shirt collar to his lion's head.

Then he spoke. And his words echoed through the church like cracking timber, fresh from the cut of an ax.

"President Lincoln once said to me that a man with few vices has even fewer virtues. I responded by saying that the Negro people were well acquainted with the vices of presidents but would be patient and wait for the new President's virtuous deeds to overtake his many failings."

The applause was swift, making ear-splitting sounds in the rafters of the church.

"Our patience has been rewarded, if only in part, by Lincoln's Emancipation Proclamation!"

There was more applause but not as loud as before.

"I know you ask yourselves, what if anything do we owe a gov-

ernment whose crimes against us are too numerous to cata-
logue? But I am not here to recount our dreaded past! I am here
to propose a way for us to create the future! I have here," he
said, holding a stack of papers above his head, "the living pre-
sent, in the form of recruitment applications! If you put your
mark on this paper, you will be taking the first step toward plac-
ing your destiny in your own hands! Most of what we've done
with our hands has enriched someone else's crop. Now we have
an opportunity to tend our own. And it's right here!" he said,
shaking the papers in his hand again. "If we take hold of the pre-
sent, the future is within our grasp!"

After his speech, Douglass passed out recruitment forms.
People pressed in all around him, and it was a while before Jim
was able to get near enough to speak to him.

"Mister Douglass," he said, after taking one of the forms, "you
really think we gonna get to fight?"

"The war cannot be won without us," Douglass said, as his
eyes zeroed in on Jim. "I've seen you before. What's your name?"

"Jim Crow."

"The dancer?"

Jim nodded.

"Do you intend to enlist?"

"I'm thinkin on it."

"If you did, many of our people might follow your example."

"I don't think so, Mister Douglass. I'm not somebody colored
people gonna pay much mind to, one way or the other."

The fire in Douglass's eyes simmered, making him seem more
relaxed.

"To be perfectly honest, Mister Crow, I have often been puz-
zled by your popularity among our people and have wondered
whether your dancing in minstrel shows has done our race more
harm than good. But in recent years, to my surprise, I've been
hearing people say the same thing about me....I guess that's
what happens when you're around long enough to have lived

108

through even worse times than those younger than yourself can remember. Some people never forgive you for having survived. Maybe they're right, Mister Crow. The longer we live, the more we should have to answer for."

Jim didn't know if he understood all of what Douglass had said. But he did know that at some point while Douglass spoke, his eyes moved away from him and seemed to be looking for something far in the distance.

There were many different versions of the events which sparked the six days of rioting that started on July 12, 1863. The most popular was the story of about one hundred young toughs, led by a cellar-digger named Patrick Merry, who burned down a building on Broadway and Twenty-ninth Street where the draft office was located. The firemen called to the scene were stoned, even though many of them were against the draft. But what got everybody falling out laughing was when they found out that the name of the fire engine company was—The Black Joke.

What had started out earlier in the day as a protest against the new draft law ended up by nightfall as a free-for-all, led by roving bands of young white men who attacked anybody they thought was to blame for the dead end their lives had come to.

Jim, Zulema, and Jubilee were at The Jig when a window was broken by a rock. Shaughnessy reached for the club he kept behind the bar, went to the door, and opened it.

"If you want somethin, why don't you come through the front door like everybody else?"

"It ain't nothin 'gainst you personal, Shaughnessy," a man said.

"It's personal when you break one a my windows!"

"We come for the niggers that dance while white men die."

"Far as I can see, none a you is dead or dyin. Now if one a you break another one a my windows, I wouldn't wager on you livin long enough for some Reb to blow you to shit!"

"We got no quarrel with you, Shaughnessy."

"You don't want no quarrel with me neither!"

"You one of us. But the way you let em have the run a the place, it's like you sidin with them."

"I'm through jaw-jackin. The next time any a you come in here, I want the money for the window on the bar."

Shaughnessy stepped back inside and bolted the door. He looked around, picking out Jim, Zulema, Jubilee, and a few other blacks.

"I won't be able to keep em off you much longer."

"You want us to leave, just say so," Jubilee said.

"What I want is for my place not to get burned down!"

"So what can we do to help, Mister Shaughnessy?" Zulema asked, in a voice seasoned with spite.

"Over here!" Shaughnessy said, directing them to come behind the bar.

He bent over and lifted up a section of the floor.

"This leads under the street. I ain't sure where it comes out at. You'll have to take your chances."

"Thanks, Shaughnessy," Jim said as he went down the steps.

Jubilee was the last one to leave and smiled at Shaughnessy as he went by him.

"I hope you're still smilin when this is over," Shaughnessy said.

"I hope so too. The last time I stopped, I killed somebody," Jubilee said, and pulled the trap door down behind him.

They trudged through the waste and muck that spewed out of busted sewer pipes, and the terrible stench brought up the taste of the last thing they'd eaten to the back of their throats. When the foul smells and their soaking wet clothes got too much for them to take, they broke up into two groups and made their way back up to the street.

Jim, Zulema, and Jubilee found themselves on the East Side, just below Fourteenth Street. Buildings were being swallowed up by flames, but there was a skin-crawling quiet that hung in the air.

A crowd had gathered in a square and was looking up at a show of some kind. Jim, Zulema, and Jubilee moved to the edge of the crowd, but all they could see was the upper body of a black man going through the motions of the strangest dance Jim had ever seen. He flailed about like he was trying to keep from drowning. Jim had never seen a dancer who could make people believe he was sinking while standing on solid ground.

Suddenly, all the life dropped out of the man's head, shoulders, and arms. It was then that Jim realized the man wasn't being held up by the platform below but from a rope above!

Zulema screamed! The crowd turned as one person, their faces torn apart with anger over the way she'd broken the spell of what was for them the greatest show they'd ever seen. The women and children at the back of the crowd were the first to attack them. Zulema was knocked to the ground and got lost underneath kicks and hands closed around sticks and stones. Jim and Jubilee tried to pull Zulema out from her attackers but they couldn't free her. Jubilee pulled out a knife and jabbed and slashed away at the women and children who were beating her. But it was too late. Men were closing in on them and Jubilee ended up fighting with Jim to get him away from the mob.

They ran and fought their way out of the clutches of many gangs of men. Jim found himself watching the way Jubilee went to battle with danger. Whether it was stabbing or swiping at someone with his knife, twisting an arm around the back until it snapped, or giving a crushing kick between someone's legs, Jubilee moved like an acrobat and looked as if he was having the time of his life.

They made their way north through Manhattan, moving like fugitive slaves. They found out that blacks weren't the only ones under attack. Anyone connected with the draft law or seen as profiting from the war was fair game for gangs who torched buildings, dished out vicious beatings, and sometimes killed.

Jubilee and Jim saw a lot of well-dressed white men beaten up. Jim passed one of them lying in the street with his head hanging like it was off the hinge. His face had been bashed in and the lenses of his glasses were crushed into his eyes.

By nightfall, Jim and Jubilee made their way into Central Park, where large numbers of blacks had gone to hide out. They rested among the trees and thick brush, but weariness still heaved in their lungs.

"What's wrong with you?" Jubilee asked, trying to break the silence between them.

"I was thinking bout Zulema."

Jubilee laughed.

"Should a thought about her when you could a done her some good."

"What you mean? You the one pulled me away when I was tryin to help her."

"That's right! Cause neither one of us was willin to kill none a them white women and children. If we had, she'd be here right now. Think about it, Jimbo. If you do, you gotta laugh."

"I don't see nothin funny!"

"I guess not, if you feelin guilty bout somethin it's too late to do anythin about. But one day you gonna get past that and see the situation for what it was....We was thinkin more about not hurtin them white folks than savin Zulema. To live with myself after that, I gotta laugh. You will too, if you got any sense!"

"That's easy for you to say. She didn't save you from …"

"That's right! From ME! And I saved YOU from them! Like I said. You gotta laugh."

Jim couldn't bring himself to laugh along with Jubilee and didn't say anything for a while.

"With a name like Jubilee, I reckon there ain't no other way for you to be. How you come by a name like that anyway?"

"I named myself. I never knew who my people was. I was one of a bunch of children on this Virginia plantation whose people was sold off or killed. My first memory was bein in the fields. I don't remember nothin before that. Once I got some size on me I knew one thing: that one day I was gon put as much gone as I could between me and that place. So I played the fool, did the darky, acted the coon, put on the mask, did whatever it took to get me to the good side of the white folks. I figured I'd get so good at it, one day somebody'd look the other way just long

113

enough for me to get long gone. Course all the other colored folks didn't have no use for me. Which was fine with me cause I didn't need nobody but me....Funny thing is—the day I plan to run off, the overseer just won't let me be. Nothin I do—skinnin, grinnin, scratchin, shufflin, or shuckin—can get him to take his eyes off me. Finally I drag him into this corn field, grab him by the throat, and squeeze the life out a him while I'm laughin in his face....His eyes was still fixed on me even after he was dead. So I had to close em with my fingers....When I got to freedom, I remembered this old woman back on the plantation talkin about what a jubilation it was gonna be when freedom came. Well, freedom didn't come. I went out and got it! That was my jubilation. And from that day I was Jubilee....I think about that overseer sometimes. He's the only white folk I couldn't fool no matter what I did. And I end up havin to kill him....Just ain't no way for me to stop laughin, Jim. Some folks laugh to keep from cryin. I laugh to keep from killin."

In one of the clearings in the park, Jubilee and Jim met up with some other blacks who sat around a cooking fire, talking about all the killing that had gone on.

"They burned down the colored orphanage," a man said.

"I saw a colored woman beat to the ground with a baby in her arms," a woman said. "A man yanked the baby away from her, took out a gun and blew its brains out."

They shook their heads slowly.

"We ain't the only ones," a man said. "They killin anybody what gets in their way."

"Yeah, but they goin OUT their way to kill us!"

"Looks like the deep North ain't no different from the deep South."

"You ain't never lied!"

Jim and Jubilee stayed in Central Park until the army put an end to the killing, burning, and looting. The bodies of the more than one hundred dead were laid out behind the police precinct houses in the areas where they were killed. Jim went back to East Fourteenth Street where he'd last seen Zulema. At a nearby police station, bodies were lined up in rows and separated into male and female.

Jim looked for Zulema among rows of women. He wanted to get the worst that could've happened out of the way first. After being sickened to the point of throwing up from pulling back the sheets from several bodies, he found her.

There was a plum-colored bruise above her left eye. But it was the rest of her face that iced him to the bone. Zulema's wide-open eyes seemed to be in the middle of seeing something that they never finished looking at. Her lips were curled into her gums and her teeth were locked together like a mad dog.

"I wouldn't pull that sheet back no farther if I were you. It ain't a pretty sight," a policeman said, who'd stopped to watch.

"Not a pretty sight!" Jim cried out, on the edge of tears. "Ain't bein dead ugly enough for you!"

The policeman shrugged and walked away.

Jim didn't look any further for the wounds that took Zulema's life. Her face was wound enough. He remembered how the crowd was so caught up in the black man's losing battle against the rope, and how he believed the man was dancing and not dangling. Zulema's scream kept her from turning into the kind of human being who could watch a man lynched without making a sound. And she paid for the sound she made with her life. But Jim, like everyone else who watched, would pay for keeping quiet. Maybe Jubilee was right after all, he thought. When you stopped being able to scream, laugh, cry, or make any noise, killing was all there was left.

Jim left the Five Points district and moved further north on the West Side of Manhattan. One morning while washing clothes along the rocky shore of the Hudson River, he saw a Union soldier watching him from a distance. He didn't pay any mind until the soldier started beating out rhythms against the rocks with his boots. Jim stopped scrubbing his britches when he knew the man had to be Jack Diamond.

"When'd you do that?" Jim asked, as Diamond got closer to him.

"You mean this?" he said, pulling on his coat.

"Yeah."

"Day before yesterday."

"So what you aim to do now?"

"Keep it on long enough so I can take it off for good."

"Wearin that ain't gonna keep what was done to folks durin the riots from happenin again."

"You wasn't talkin like that a few months ago."

"I wasn't seein then the way I'm seein now."

"So what you gonna do?"

"I don't know. But wearin a uniform ain't gonna be no part of it."

"You been around The Jig lately?" Diamond asked.

"That's all over with."

"What do you mean?"

"Dancin. I don't think I got it in me no more."

"I don't believe that. You may not feel up to it. But you still got it in you."

"When you leavin?" Jim asked.

"In the mornin."

"Well, when you get right down to it, marchin ain't all that different from dancin."

"I don't know what else I can do," Diamond said.

"I guess lettin somebody else tell you what to do is better than doin nothin."

"Like you?"

"Yeah. Like me," Jim said, laughing.

"It's funny. I joined up thinkin that's what you was gonna do. And here you go, still side-steppin me like always. I should a known better than to try and figure what you was gonna do next."

"Jack, you know how it goes. First your money, then your clothes."

"Yeah. I guess our kind of act is just about done for," Diamond said.

"Ours ain't the only one. When the war's over, the whole country's gonna have to come up with a new act."

"Well," Diamond said, "nobody can say we didn't give a good account of ourselves. Probably better than most."

Jim gathered up his clothes and they walked across the stone-paved shoreline of the Hudson River toward the road. The footing made walking slow going and every step was an adventure. As they struggled between a stumble and a fall, their feet couldn't help but remember the steps of an old routine where they turned the stage into a floating log. And then, for what was probably the last time, they flirted with falling but kept their balance in the only way they could in a country that had already taken a terrible fall.

The rumors spread like a cold that everybody was catching whenever somebody else sneezed. There was no better proof that the stories were true than the large number of blacks arriving in New York City after fleeing the South. Early in 1865, blacks met regularly in churches, halls, taverns, the streets, and in the homes of abolitionists. But wherever they got together, the talk was about how little time there was left for a war killing its way to an end.

The end came for Jack Diamond in a place called Spotsylvania. What was left of him was found in a pile of arms, legs, and headless torsos. Like many of the men who died that day in May of 1864, Diamond had written his name on a slip of paper and pinned it to his pants. Since his legs were the only parts of his body ever found, that slip of paper was the only way he was identified. The story of what was left of Jack Diamond became grist for the mill in the legend of the greatest jig dancer ever to heist his legs! And each time Jim heard another version of the story, the loss of Jack Diamond didn't weigh on him so heavily.

Jim stood at Fourteenth Street watching the parades and celebrations moving up Broadway. He had known where he was as soon as he got there. It was almost the same spot where the black man had been lynched and Zulema was beaten to death. A number of horse-drawn wagons filled with men moved toward Jim. There were stacks of sabers in each wagon that men waved and then broke over their knees to the cheers of the crowds along the street.

From the other direction a large group of blacks and whites walked behind a horse-drawn hearse. Jim couldn't understand why the people seemed so full of fun while they walked with death in a carriage. Even the wagon train of men breaking swords slowed down out of respect for what everybody thought was a funeral march.

A black woman and man climbed on top of the carriage and held a broken shackle and chain above their heads. As the hearse and the lead wagon loaded with men and swords came up alongside each other, both marches stopped. The men in the wagons were no longer breaking sabers, and except for children who were playing circle games, the crowds on both sides of the street had stopped shouting. The woman on top of the hearse looked down at one of the men in the lead wagon and held up the shackle.

"Slavery's dead!" she said.

"But you niggers ain't!" the man said.

There was a second or two when no one seemed to be breathing. But then, like the cannon fire that started the war, voices exploded in the streets. The wheels of the hearse and the lead wagon rocked back and forth as the drivers pulled the reins to stop the horses from rearing up. Then the two parades moved forward again in the direction that the other had just come from.

Many in the streets fell in behind the hearse while others followed the men in the wagons who were no longer breaking swords but were waving them. Those who didn't follow either line of march argued over what had been said by the woman and the man.

The whirlwind of noise made Jim feel like clouds were gathering in his head. He started to rock back on his heels and decided to sit down to steady himself. And while waiting for his head to clear, Jim watched some children, their arms linked in a circle, moving backward and forward in time like the hands on a runaway clock.

PART 2

Jim Crow left New York City by wagon and headed West with Jubilee and some other actors, looking for a traveling show to hitch onto. The countryside was cut to pieces like something butchered on a chopping block. The only crops to be seen were the bones of the war dead. A day didn't pass without Jim seeing blacks digging up a field and lugging away wheelbarrows loaded with skulls.

Cities and towns were in total ruin. From a distance, streaks of sunlight cut through buildings beaten to the bones by cannon fire. Their wagon creaked through each city, and the skeletons of buildings reached up around them like hacked-up letters of the alphabet.

Jim left the others when they reached Louisville. He told them he would see them in St. Louis after he found out if his mother was alive, dead, or lost forever. He left the wagon within sight of the old slave quarters surrounding the Churchill mansion. While making his way to the cabin Whisper had lived in, he saw Union soldiers coming in and out of the mansion.

When he got to the cabin, there were mostly women, children, and a few old men sitting in front. They stared at him the way someone might look at a hitching post.

"How do?" Jim said to no one in particular.

Some nodded, but most kept whatever was going on behind their faces under lock and key.

"I'm lookin for someone who used to live here. Some a you might know her. Name was Whisper."

Something stirred up in the faces of a few women who would've been around Whisper's age if she were still alive.

"What's yours?" a woman asked, her words following something she'd spit out of her mouth.

"Jim."

"That all the name you got?"

"Crow."

Two of the women looked at each other like they were thinking the same thing.

"You that dancin man?"

"Used to be. Like the woman I'm lookin for used to live here. She's my mama."

"I knew her," a woman said, "but I don't know what become of her after she got sold off."

The woman turned in the direction of the other women but they shook their heads.

"You might wanna talk to the Yankees. They might have some paper on her."

"Thank you," Jim said, turning to leave.

"How come you say you used to be a dancer?" a woman asked.

"Cause I don't do it no more."

"Why not?"

"Seems like it got to where it did me more harm than good."

"It ain't none a my business," the woman said. "But if your mama's alive, she's liable to hear bout you a lot quicker than you hearin bout her, 'specially if you dancin."

"Thank you, Mam," Jim said, and walked in the direction of the old mansion.

The paint on the building that was once milky white was now cracked, flaky, and smudged to a smoky gray. Union soldiers stood around picking at their faces and pulling on their uniforms. The soldier at the front door asked Jim to state his business and seemed excited that he had something to do. He did an about-face and led Jim inside.

Most of the furniture was covered with bedsheets. The officers dragged their feet through the house like they were half-asleep. Jim knocked on the door of the officer who was in charge.

"What is it now?" said the voice behind the door.

Jim opened the door and saw a man whose face was covered by a briar bush of a beard.

"What do you want?"

Jim paused long enough to see the papers scattered all over the officer's desk and a world-weary look in his eyes.

"I'm lookin for my mama. She was sold away from here years back."

"How far back?"

"Twenty years."

"You out a luck. I got soldiers under my command that I can't account for over the last twenty hours!"

"Ain't there no papers on slaves that was sold when Churchill owned the place?"

"If there are, they were destroyed or taken before we got here."

"Thank you much for your time," Jim said, turning to go.

"I wish I could be of more help," the officer said, "but a lot a people got lost in this way—the living as well as the dead."

Jim had never been inside the Churchill mansion, so before he left, he stopped to look at the shapes of the furniture that were covered up by the sheets. Some of the pieces of furniture had the shapes of animals and trees.

"You wanna see what's underneath?"

Jim jerked his head around and saw the officer he'd spoken to a few minutes before.

"No sir. I was just lookin."

"You gotta right to more than that. Who knows? Maybe something in here was bought with money from the sale of your mother!"

Then the officer started yanking the sheets off everything in the room. The other soldiers stopped their sleepwalking to watch. Every time Jim heard the flapping sound of a sheet when the officer pulled it off, he couldn't believe what he saw: a dining table almost as long as the room, chairs as large as the inside of a carriage, stuffed animal heads, and bigger-than-life-size human heads made out of bronze.

"Take whatever you can carry away," the officer said.

"I wouldn't know what to do with it, sir."

"Sell it, for Christ sakes! Some of this stuff would bring you a nice little piece of money. It won't bring your mother back, but at least you'd have something to show for what this place has cost you."

Jim walked around slowly to all the uncovered pieces of furniture and statues. He moved his hands over each one and then turned to the officer.

"Thank you sir. But there's nothing here for me."

When Jim got back to the cabin, the woman who'd spoken to him before said he was welcome to stay until the train heading to St. Louis arrived. He moved around the room he once called home in a daze. Jim rubbed his hands over the floor planks where he and Whisper had slept and heard the floor creak as he walked over places where they had stood, sat, or ate.

"I didn't know how to make mention of it when you first come," the woman said. "But the last time I saw her, she was put in the well out yonder."

"The well! Why?"

"I never knowed why. And I never saw her no more after that."

"You think she ...?" Jim said, leaping to his feet.

"Naw. There ain't nothin but rain water and vermin been in there for years."

Jim ran outside and stopped a few feet from the well. He ran his hands along the outer wooden frame and looked down into the dark and bottomless hole. What was it like for her to be down there? Was she ever taken out alive? Or was she left for the rats to eat out her eyes? How did she sound as her songs, prayers, moans, and cries tore out of her throat and reached up out of the darkness? Did anyone hear her?

Jim straddled the mouth of the well, clawed at the insides, and pulled at the roots of anything growing that he could grip. Was this the closest he would get to whatever life she had left after the last time he saw her? If so, he wanted to hold onto as much of it as he could. Jim opened his mouth and started to breathe deeply, taking in the smell of the damp earthen moss from inside the well. He screamed down into the darkness and heard his voice echo back to him from the same bottom that Whisper's cries had come out of.

It took several men to pry Jim loose from the well and get him back to the cabin.

"How you be?" the woman asked, after Jim had calmed himself.

"Looks like I kind a lost myself out there for a while."

"But you found what you was lookin for."

"I guess this is close as I'm gonna get."

"That's more than most folks can say who lost their people."

"She used to always tell me, every goodbye ain't gone."

"Well, now that the goodbye is back, you think you can give some a your dance to us who remember and some to the rest who too young to know?"

A place on the floor was cleared for him. He stepped into the space and lifted one foot and then the other. His feet clapped against the floor, and he jabbed with his hands like a boxer. A crowd gathered outside the cabin, crowding in front of the door and looking through the windows. Those who couldn't see made do with listening.

The smell of Jim's own sweat filled his nostrils and memories moistened into tears. He was not aware of much else after that except shivering in a corner of the cabin with a blanket wrapped around his sweat-soaked body.

Jim waited for the train to St. Louis and thought about being free. He wondered if it sometimes meant not finding what you lose. And if it did, could it also mean finding what you never had?

On the train to St. Louis, Jim noticed two women who had just about everybody in the car latched onto everything they said. Both had parts stretching through their thick black hair whose color was a shade darker than the apple-butter brown of their faces.

"Who're those two women everybody payin so much attention to?" Jim asked a man sitting across the aisle.

"They the Featherstone Sisters."

"You mean the ones that got their own traveling show?"

"That's them."

Jim had heard about them and by all accounts, Starletta and Violet Featherstone could do it all: from introducing all the acts in a minstrel show to taking on the male roles of Mister Tambo and Mister Bones and any other part that wasn't spoken for. They'd had trouble keeping a company of their own together because the public, white as well as black, was not ready for the spectacle of women performing in and running their own traveling shows. They took the brunt of all the trouble that went with being women in a world that was mostly made up of men. But the Featherstones had a reputation for being more than up to the task of dealing with men, as Jim found out as he watched them holding forth in a group of men at the other end of the car.

"A woman just wasn't meant to do the same things as a man," one of the men said.

Starletta Featherstone pressed the palms of her hands across her forehead, cat-cradled her legs so her dress stretched tightly between her knees, and wiped the moisture from her hands into the part of her dress covering her thighs.

"You right," she said. "But I'd even go you one better than

126

that. I don't think you men should be doin half the stuff I see you doin. So I definitely hope I don't live to see women trying to imitate some of the low-life carryin on I've seen from you men."

"Like what?"

"Now I know you don't want me to get started on how some of you right here in this Jim Crow car have on occasion been so twisted with drink, you've tried to get favors of the flesh from livestock!"

"That ain't what I mean," the man said, but had to wait for the laughter to die down before he could explain himself. "I'm talkin bout the saying that goes that when woman's rights is stirred a bit, the first reform she bitches on is how she can with least delay draw a pair of britches on!"

Many of the men in the car nodded in agreement. The feeling was not new but most had never heard it put in quite that turn of phrase before. Starletta held her breath to take note of the challenge before jumping back into the scuffle.

"Puttin on britches ain't never made nobody a man. I always thought they was just a change a clothes, myself. As a matter of fact, I've never heard the men I know talk about wanting to be men!"

"If you wasn't a woman, I'd ..."

"Yeah, I know. And I wouldn't a said it if you was really a man."

The man's eyebrows raised into two curved moon slivers. He started to get up from his seat and Starletta thought about the straight razor she kept strapped to her thigh. But a hand fell on the man's shoulder that made him think twice about getting up.

" 'Cuse me, Miss Featherstone. My name's Jim Crow. I been hearin about you and your sister's act for a good while now. I always wondered how y'all got started in this business, being that there ain't too many women that got the gumption for this kind a life."

SO THIS WAS JIM CROW! Starletta liked the way he filled out his clothes and the fact that his pants and coat were worn in spots. There was something nice about a man whose clothes made you think about his body. Standing with his jacket open, swept back on the left side by his hand resting on his hip, Starletta couldn't take her eyes off Jim's wrist. It was the set of the bone wrapped in flesh with a design made by his veins that snatched Starletta's breath away.

"I'd be only too glad to tell on myself, Mister Crow, if you'd return the favor."

"Turnabout is only fair play," he said.

"All right then. Courtesy of Mister Crow, the rest of y'all get yourselves a story....Part a the reason travelin is so agreeable to Violet and me is that my mother was carryin us when she and my father escaped slavery in Mississippi. All along the way to freedom, they were taken in by people who hid them till it was safe to move on. And everywhere they stopped, they would tell about their travels. Now, these folks they met along the way must a heard plenty stories from runaways, being that they was part a the Underground Railroad transportin people to freedom. But my mother and father had a way of tellin how somethin happened that had folks puttin their hands underneath their chins, makin whoever was listenin feel there was room for them in whatever they was hearin. By the time we got to Ohio, there was a trail a stories followin us from other people who escaped after we did. They would come to where we lived, askin after the stories they heard on their way to freedom.

"At first people would come to the house to listen to our folks. But it got so people would come around at all hours. So, my folks would get everybody together one day a week, just like church, and meet at somebody's house and tell stories they'd heard and others they'd made up. Pretty soon they got to be more reliable than a newspaper. Instead a tellin people how somethin happened, they told how it felt.

"After Violet and me was born and got some age on us, our folks started gettin requests to go to other parts of the state. Neither of them was bothered by all the time we spent on the road, cause havin escaped slavery, they was never that comfortable in one place for very long anyway. So there was always this natural hankerin to move on, to disguise themselves, and tell lies more barefaced than a baby's backside. It was all part of makin them feel more secure in their freedom....Next thing you know, we known as the Featherstone Traveling Theatre and we're performin all over free territory. When our folks died some years back, Violet and me kept it goin, not just out a loyalty to them but cause this is all we ever really wanted to do."

There were some in the car who were held captive by Starletta's gift for storytelling. But there were others whose faces were as cold as a winter chill over the fact that they were in the presence of Jim Crow. And finally, there was the frown that wouldn't leave Violet Featherstone's face as she watched flirtation drift back and forth between her sister and Jim. While Starletta spoke, Violet sat with her arms folded. She couldn't see what Starletta saw in him. Anybody could tell he was putting on an act.

The group that had closed around Starletta and Violet went back to their seats. But Jim stayed and asked could he join them. It was only after they'd talked for a while that he noticed more about them than their likeness as twins. Words were more playful in Starletta's mouth, while Violet's talk broke into brittle pieces of mockery.

"Thanks for what you did a while back," Starletta said. "That could've gotten ugly."

"He knew he was wrong. But he'd gone too far and needed somebody to help him get out of it without makin him look too bad. It just happened to be me."

"Since you on the subject, tell us somethin about you."

"Not much to tell that ain't already been told."

"You Jim Crow?" a voice asked above him. He looked up and saw a group of men staring down at him like they were about to tell him that somebody had up and died.

"That's my name but not my address."

"Maybe not for you. But it's where the rest of us live," the man said.

"That ain't my doin."

"It started with you."

"You got your people mixed up. Ain't nothing started with me 'cept what I made up myself. And even that ain't all my own doin."

"It don't matter if it ain't all your doin," another man said.

Jim knew there wasn't anything he could say to make things right. There was no end to it: this need people had to always have somebody to blame and to be more worried about what someone else was doing than what they could do themselves. And since these men weren't interested in taking any of the weight for the way they'd been Jim Crowed, Jim wasn't about to take it for them.

"I'm a go back to the porter car and see a friend of mine," he said to Starletta and Violet, before getting up and pushing past the men in the aisle who moved out of his way almost as quick as they'd gotten in it.

"What do you make of him?" Violet asked.

"What I make of him don't seem to be the point," Starletta said.

"Why not? He puts on his pants one leg at a time, like any other man."

"There may be more to him than that."

"How you know?"

"You seem to forget, Violet. We once had a daddy!"

"I ain't forgot nothin. Especially, what we've always gotten from men and women!"

"Maybe I need a change."

"I know what you need. You ain't no different from me. You still wanna make sure you do the pickin. And you know as well as I do that gettin picked don't make a man special. It makes him lucky!"

The way Starletta acted with Jim Crow went against everything

130

Violet was used to. Over the years, they'd both figured out how to have their fill of men and women without getting eaten up themselves. The dim view most people had of women being with women made it easier for Violet and Starletta to have love affairs without worrying about some female wrapping her life around them like a corset.

Men were a whole other matter. Violet and Starletta had been around enough men to know that most of them were always hot to trot but not for very long. And those who could trot a little longer only wanted to ride so they could brag about it and cover up how afraid these two women made them feel.

To protect themselves, Violet and Starletta never made love with a man except during the bloody part of the month—when their desire was strongest and getting pregnant wasn't as likely. And for those men who tried to get ugly, they both kept a straight razor strapped to a thigh.

Starletta and Violet shared just about everything. They never even let the desire for the same woman or man come between them because WHAT they were doing was always more important than WHO they were doing it with. But now, Starletta seemed more interested in WHO this man Crow was than in WHAT he could do for her. And Violet was fearful that a time might come when she would lose Starletta and have to go it alone in the only way she could live in a world with other people.

Jim found Daddy Joe stretched out on his bunk in the Pullman porter car. He was big enough to take up the space of two men and was known for being able to make up an upper and lower berth at the same time. But even that didn't cause as much of a stir as an incident some years before at a water stop. Indians waylaid the train and would have made short work of everyone on board if it hadn't been for Daddy Joe, who parlayed with them in their own lingo and made them a gift of all the famous Pullman blankets. As the train moved farther west, the passengers shivered through cold evenings but couldn't stop talking about what Daddy Joe had done. Since Daddy Joe knew what it was like to have his life blown up even bigger than his body, he was one of the few people that Jim could talk to.

All the porters were asleep on their bunks except Daddy Joe and two men studying their next move to outfox the other on a checkerboard.

"Thought I'd come by and sit for a while," Jim said, sitting on the end of Daddy Joe's bunk.

"What's doin?" Daddy Joe asked, moving legs the size of logs to the floor.

"Just come from talkin to the Featherstone Sisters."

"They somethin more than a little light sport."

"Yeah! Some a the fellas was givin em a hard time."

"Well, it comes with the birth cry. But from what I hear, they can hold their ground as good as any man!"

"You got that right! The one called Starletta can make a sucker shut up! She had this joker so turned around he couldn't come out his mouth straight."

"Now that's somethin I wish I'd seen."

"A few started in on me again."

"Blamin you for their shame?"

"What else?"

"Like I said before bout the birth cry …"

"It ever bother you that folks give you credit for things you never did?" Jim asked.

"Yeah, it bothers me! Cause even things in your favor have a way a turnin against you when folks start blamin you for what they used to praise you for."

"It's kind a funny when you think on it. There was a time when the Jim Crow car was somethin special to colored folks."

"Still is," Daddy Joe said.

"But not in the same way."

"That's the trouble with being special when it's on somebody else's say so….Those stories about me tradin with Indians and makin two beds at once had me believin I was runnin on the same stuff they feed this train engine. Now I ain't denyin those things happened. But I'm through spicin em up just to make me feel better about myself."

"I've done some a that," Jim said. "In some ways, I understand colored folks blamin me for the way they been Jim Crowed."

"Maybe one day, more of us'll come up with a gospel according to us and stop swearin by what comes out a white folks' mouths just cause they say it's holy!"

"Now that would be somethin special!" Jim said.

Someone came in from the front of the car, and the sound of wheel against rail rattled in their ears for the seconds it took to open and close the door.

"Thought I'd find you here," said a man, whose enormous clean-shaven head took up over half the space between his shoulders.

"Hey, Two-Faced," Jim said.

"How you, Jim? Saw you talkin to the Featherstones. They tell you bout the new show they puttin together when they get to St. Louis?"

"No."

"Well? What you think?"

"It don't have nothin to do with me."

"Ain't that why you goin to St. Louis? To sign on with their show?"

"Two-Faced, you must have a lotta time on your hands to be studyin about what I'm gonna do."

"It's just that me and some a the fellas saw you talkin to em and was wonderin if that's what it was about—cause if it was, maybe you could put in a good word for us."

"Why don't you talk to them yourself?"

"They don't know me from nobody. But they know you!"

"I can't tell em who to put in their show."

"Why? Cause I do black face?"

"It ain't got nothin to do with that."

"In a pig shit it don't. I know all about you. You think you too good for blackin up....I ain't the dancer you is, Jim. But nobody gave me a way out a slavery and set me up in my own private car. I had to find my own way out and leg it the best way I could. I know blackin up is US DOIN WHITE FOLKS DOIN US! But minstrelsy ain't the only place where that goes on. Like most of our people, I know I gotta stretch the truth in order to live. But long as WE know what we doin, it don't matter what white folks think!"

"Two-Faced, you ain't gotta explain yourself to me."

"You know, Jim, you got so much ass on your shoulders, one a these days you gonna break your fuckin neck!"

The sound of hammering steel and air pressure rushed into the car again as Two-Faced opened and closed the door behind him. Jim leaned back against the wooden column connecting the top and bottom bunk and traded a look with Daddy Joe.

"Yeah, I know," Jim said. "It comes with the birth cry."

Because St. Louis was close to the Mississippi River, thousands of blacks from Arkansas, Mississippi, and Louisiana made their way there after the Civil War. Men and women, who'd never been outside the plantation they were born on, couldn't wait to find out what the rest of the world was like. And black women, traveling alone, made up a large number of the people who ended up in this river city on the Mississippi.

On one side of the railroad yard lay the main arteries of St. Louis and on the other side there were roadhouses that served an all-black clientele. Black women who were new to the city and with no place to stay usually found lodging at the only boarding house for women. It was run by Charmaine Cusseaux who had come to St. Louis from Louisiana at the end of the war. She'd lived with a man in Louisiana, but when he decided to stay, she left without him. Arriving in St. Louis by riverboat, she met a gambler. With his skill at games of chance and her ability to take a small grubstake and turn it into a much larger bundle of cash, they opened up one of the more successful roadhouses on the black side of the tracks. But like some men coming out of slavery, the gambler had a strong crush on danger and didn't give much thought to playing it safe. One night he was stabbed to death in a senseless argument over the deal of a hand in a card game.

Wanting to get into a business where blood and brawling weren't part of making a living, Charmaine took what she'd earned from her fling with the gambler and opened a boarding-house. It became a place where black women stayed who came from all over the deep South. When black men talked about why these women had come to St. Louis, they poked a finger into their chests. While this may have been true in some cases, the women who resided at Charmaine's often said they were in St. Louis for their own pleasure, which didn't have to include men. When this got back to the men, they had a good laugh and agreed that these women only wanted the company of other women. What they seemed to miss was that the women living in this scandalous house could be bold enough to believe they could have both.

Charmaine sat on the porch of her house with her regular boarders and those who'd arrived by train earlier that day. Fleshy, the color of eggnog, she was anxious to talk to Starletta and Violet who she hadn't seen in months.

"Has the world been treatin you or have you been doin the treatin?" she asked.

"A bit of both," Starletta said. "Most folks still ain't standin or sittin for much of what we got in mind for the stage. But they want us to lay down for just about anything!"

"Y'all must have plenty backbone up the brain by now, all the years you've had to get your backs up for all that abuse."

"Speakin of havin your back up, what about you, Charmaine?" Violet asked. "You still gettin grief over not lettin women have no male company past midnight who don't pass mustard with you?"

"Somebody always squawk but they respect it. You know I'd be the last one to try 'n stop any woman from answerin the call of nature," Charmaine said, resting her hand on Violet's knee and poking her cheek out from the inside with her tongue to keep from smiling. "But there's many that come through here that ain't much more than girls. I've seen too many end up lookin at the world from their backs on a regular basis cause they didn't have no place to stay when they got here. They need some law laid down to em, so if they decide to break it, they'll have to go to some trouble. And if they ain't ready to do that, then dawn don't need to catch em in the company of no man. At least not in my house, it don't."

136

There was a long silence as fear started to blister the bark and the bite of the women on the porch. Some remembered the times when they let the day following the night before catch them with a strange man; and they were left feeling surer than spit that the only thing that changed was not the kind of men they ended up with but the sky that came with the daybreak.

"What else been goin on since we was here last?" Starletta asked.

"The biggest thing was this all-colored minstrel show that passed through here some months back. When folks came to see the show, the actors Jim Crowed the theatre by settin up an all-white section in the balcony. The white folks pitched a fit, 'specially when none a the colored gave up their seats down below on the first floor. Damn near had a riot till folks in the show cooled things down by tellin the white folks they was seated in the balcony so they could look down on the colored like they was used to doin. But if they didn't like it that way, the blacks could go back to sittin in the balcony and look down on them....Everybody, white and colored, near about busted a gut laughin at that. But the show left town the next day. I guess they didn't wanna wait around too long for the joke to wear off on the white folks."

"I hope folks in these parts are ready for the joke that me and Violet gonna play on em," Starletta said.

"Oh?" Charmaine said.

"We gonna put together a new show, open to anyone who's got somethin special to offer."

"Women too?"

"That's right!"

"I don't know if anybody, black or white, gonna be ready for that," Charmaine said.

"Nobody's ever ready for somethin they not used to," Starletta said. "But that don't mean they won't watch....We met the one and only Jim Crow on the train the other day. Now tell me, who was ever ready for him? He's been dogged by everybody at one time or another. But I bet if we got him to join the show, there wouldn't be an empty seat in the house. And you know why? Cause people are more interested in what they don't like than anything else....Of course, like that show you was just talkin about, we gotta be careful. Folks can get mean when they think they enjoyin somethin they ain't supposed to like. But that's why I love travelin shows. Cause you can always get away with a lot more on a stage than you can in the street."

"Seems like you also tryin to get away with not tellin Charmaine that your interest in Jim Crow ain't strictly business," Violet said.

"That's because what I choose to tell her is strictly my business!" Starletta said.

Charmaine could tell that the words passing between them were not as playful as their digs at one another usually were. It took her by surprise. And she couldn't wait to meet the man who'd come between them.

Jim had finished eating breakfast and was sitting in the front room of the roadhouse where he and Jubilee were staying. He spent the better part of Sunday morning watching blacks on their way to church and seeing more than a few whose walk was soggy from the drunken slosh of Saturday night. By midday, churchgoers, who'd gotten a good talking to, passed Saturday night merrymakers who were walking off what wouldn't take talking to. Some of those same good-timers lived at the roadhouse. Jim could hear footdragging coming from the floor above. He looked up when what sounded like several pairs of weighted-down feet dragged down the stairs.

Jubilee and three other men slumped into chairs near his. Jim was still surprised at how glad he was to see Jubilee. This was the same man who might've beaten him to death if Zulema hadn't stopped him. He was also the man who saved him from a lynch mob. Jubilee was his last link to the time when he came to New York after the murder of Tom Rice. Everyone else was either dead or lost. Jim ran his finger over the scar on the side of his face.

"What's with you?" Jubilee asked.

"Just thinkin bout when we was in New York."

"You always unpackin a bag from some place other than where you at. When I met you, you'd just finished travelin with a dead man. When I left you on that road in Kentucky, you was chasin the ghost of your mama. And now you thinkin bout the place you couldn't get away from fast enough. You don't make no more sense goin than you do comin."

"I missed you too, Jubilee," Jim said, as their laughter lightened the load in all their heads. "What can I tell you, Jubilee? I'm a dancer. I can never stand still."

"Speakin of standin still, we sure ain't had much luck findin a show to get us goin again," one of the men said.

"What about them handbills all over town callin for actors to try out for the show run by those two colored women?" another man asked.

"You mean the Featherstone Sisters," Jim said.

"Ain't they the two that come in on the same train you was on?" Jubilee asked.

Jim nodded.

"You think they for real?"

"I think they mean to do what they say," Jim said.

"I ain't never worked under no women before," a man said.

"When they get a look at you, they may not wanna be over top a you neither!" Jubilee said.

"I was just wonderin how they expect to handle all the hard-heads they gonna have to put up with."

"If you that worried," Jubilee said, "then you ought a hire on with the Featherstone Sisters to keep the rest of us in line."

"You don't think they may be in over their heads?" the other man asked.

"That ain't my worry. If they can't cut it, then they ain't got no business bein out here in it," Jubilee said.

"Speakin of cuttin it," someone else said, "I hear tell both of em can cut the mustard and lick the jar better than a man!"

Jubilee saw that Jim didn't join in the laughter. He started to say something but changed his mind.

The auditions for the Featherstone Traveling Theatre were held in a theater jammed with people of every age, sex, and race. Starletta and Violet stood on stage and looked out over the audience, full of hopefuls who saw these tryouts as a chance to make up a better life than the one they walked into the theater with. And if they were lucky enough to be picked, they had the chance to be somebody else in every show.

"We don't know exactly what we're looking for," Starletta said.

"But we wanna go one better than Noah's Ark and float a show full of folks who are one of a kind! So whatever you do, if you can give us that, we'll sign you on for sure."

There were singers, dancers, and hard-working fools from every town within fifty miles. Jubilee and Two-Faced were signed on quickly. Two-Faced had everybody whooping it up, doing a routine in white face, then turning around to show his real face, which people thought was the back of his head. A white woman, who sang instead of talked, called herself Sorrow; and her voice seemed to come straight out the throat of a loon. Another woman, who could have passed for white, put a spell on the audience as she moved her knees around in their sockets with such ease that a man hollered, "Go 'head now, Sweet Knees!"

A white man named Trash used a burlap bag to show the audience how he'd always thrown himself into everything he did. So when he threw himself into a dance that he said was at the bottom of the bag, he couldn't get out of either one. Trash wasn't as talented as some of the others, but Violet and Starletta liked the way he used not getting out of the bag as a way of getting into the show. When asked if he had a last name, Trash said it was the same as his first. He also said he'd fight anybody who put 'white' anywhere near his name.

After Trash came an Indian woman who didn't speak at all. Around her neck was a piece of cardboard that had WHICH-AWAY printed on it. While everyone watched with their mouths open, she turned her back to the audience and made herself up into a man, then mixed herself up into a woman and a man and even made believe she was a horse, an ear of corn, rain, and wind.

The next man tried to eat corn on the cob with his feet but couldn't quite get it into his mouth. And one of the last to try out was a white man who said he'd been a failure in everything he'd tried in life from supporting the wrong presidents, fighting on the losing side in the war, to going through one disaster after another in every contract he ever entered into from sharecropping to marriage. But his luck changed, he said, when he changed the "i" in 'fail' to an "l" and started to 'fall' for a living at county fairs and Fourth of July celebrations. Then he showed how he did it by jumping off the balcony into the aisle of the orchestra and breaking both ankles and his collarbone.

When the last person left the stage after strutting their stuff, Starletta looked over the audience until she found Jim.

"You waitin for an invitation, Mr. Crow?"

Jim smiled from his seat several rows back.

"I'm havin such a good time I forgot all about takin a turn myself."

"Don't let him get away with that," Jubilee said. "He ain't never had a good time that got too far away from his feet."

"What about it, Mr. Crow? You gonna dance or dangle?"

Jim hadn't felt like dancing since he and Jack Diamond beat their feet on the rocky shore along the Hudson River. But something got up inside him. He jumped out of his seat and jiggled his body down the aisle to the stage, going through loose-jointed moves that made it look like he was coming apart. The ear-splitting ruckus of whistles, shouts, foot-stomping, and hand-clapping rode on the heels of every step Jim took. Starletta turned to Violet, who sighed and raised her head up like she was looking for help from above.

"We can't quarrel with what you just showed us," Starletta said, after the crowd had quieted down. "The only question I got is: Are you comin on the Ark with us or ain't you?"

"If you got a spot for a hoofer, I reckon I can fill it."

Starletta and Violet got everyone together on stage who'd been picked for their new traveling show.

"My sister and I," Violet began, "just want you to know how lucky we are to have all the talent that's here right now. We believe we've got the makings of a show that'll have people waiting in line like they do when they're drawing their pay....The only other thing we want to say is—if anyone feels that it don't sit well with them to perform under our name, it'd be better if you left now with no hard feelings and not wait for us to have to fire you later."

The weight of what many were thinking but didn't want to say settled into shoulders, backs, and necks.

"I guess that means any problems we gonna have will come out later and not sooner."

"You can't really blame nobody for not speaking up," Jubilee said. "If I'm gonna lose a job I was glad to get, it ain't gonna be for somethin I was thinkin!"

"You got problems with us bein in charge?" Violet asked.

"No! But if I did, I wouldn't tell you. You'd have to catch me in the lie."

"We were hopin everybody would feel free enough to be on the up and up."

"That's just what I'm doin. Like the freedom the government say we got, it's gonna take some time to feel free enough to tell you somethin that could cost us the jobs you just got through givin us!"

"That's not what I meant!" Violet said.

"Oh! So you got the same problem we got!"

"What's that?"

"Sayin what you don't mean!" Jubilee said, to cheers and laughter that just about shook the theater loose from its foundation.

No matter where their station in life was, people were talking about the new show that these two colored women named Featherstone had put together. Some couldn't wait to get an eyeful of this not-to-be-believed, upside-down group of folks. But there were others who saw the Featherstone Traveling Theatre as a freak show with a bunch of heathens hellbent on pulling the floor out from under the country so that no one could tell the top from the bottom. Starletta and Violet were savvy enough to keep many of their tried-and-true skits that were favorites of audiences over the years. But they weren't interested in a show made up only of scenes that had nothing to do with one another. Instead, they hit on the idea of using these skits as a breather for the audience during comedy-soaked music-dramas that were the main part of the show.

When they weren't rehearsing, Starletta and Violet spent as much time with the other actors as possible. They knew it wasn't easy keeping the peace among actors living together on the road and getting them to put out their best effort every night. And it would be even trickier with the hodgepodge make-up of this group. So Violet and Starletta decided to get up under the lid and skin of everyone who signed on. If either one of them had a strong feeling about an actor, one way or another, that would be the one they would try to get to know.

About a week before the show was to open, Charmaine threw a party for the entire company at her boardinghouse. She had done it as a favor to Violet and Starletta, but also to get all these actors together under her roof. She loved performers of any kind. They took chances and didn't complain about the way things turned out. Charmaine saw herself that way and liked to be around people who lived out their dreams in every move they made.

144

The dining and living room flooded together as people moved freely between the two. With the backs of her hands resting on her hips, Charmaine looked out over the rooms. She was pleased with herself for having opened up her house to this assbackwards acting group of folks who were enjoying the taste of each other's company as much as the taste of biscuits, fried chicken, turnip greens, yams, and pot liquor. Charmaine was also glad to have finally gotten a good look at the legendary Jim Crow. She had been in the audience when he brought the house down with his unbelievable jiggle down the aisle. Looking at him now as he stood talking with Starletta, he could've been anybody. It would be interesting to find out, she thought, if there were other things he did that made him like nobody else.

"I been meaning to ask you," Starletta said, "what made you change your mind about dancing again?"

"I really didn't have it in my mind to dance at all," Jim said. "But somethin came over me—which is the way I end up doin most things."

"It won't bother you, seeing Jubilee, Two-Faced, and some others blackin up?"

"Oh! It'll bother me. But I'll get over it!"

"Blackin up may be the least of our worries," Starletta said.

"What do you mean?"

"There's gonna be folks who're not going to like us no matter what we do."

"I been there."

"It could really get ugly."

"Least it'll be out in the open."

"Speaking of things being out in the open," Starletta said, "you interest me."

"In what way?"

"Usually, there ain't nothin a man can do to improve on what I have in mind for him."

"And what's that?"

"What do you think?"

"You tell me. You the one with the plan."

"That's just it. I ain't got one."

"That bother you?"

"With anybody else, it would. But with you, I don't wanna figure it all out ahead a time."

Violet was standing within earshot of Starletta and heard the last part of what her sister said. She shook her head and walked over to the food table and poured herself some more of Charmaine's homemade brew. Violet took a sip and shivered from the buzz it made in the back of her neck before going straight to her head!

"You shakin cause a the drink or from me gettin close to you?"

Violet jerked her head around and saw Charmaine. She'd never known anyone like Charmaine who never hid the way she felt about anything. It didn't matter whether it was sad, cruel, funny, lustful, or stupid. Charmaine found it impossible to see anything and act like she didn't see it. When she was surprised, her eyes narrowed to slits. Her nostrils spread when she was angry; she bit down on her lower lip when she was upset; and she licked her teeth when a woman got her attention.

Violet had once asked Charmaine why she'd been drawn to her and not Starletta. Charmaine said the first time she saw them perform, she felt Violet's eyes on her. She was tickled that Violet could watch her and still pay attention to what she was doing on stage. Violet remembered when Charmaine told her this after the show, it made her laugh. Something only her parents and Starletta were ever able to do.

"What's the matter? Not havin a good time?" Charmaine asked.

"I'm all right. But I ain't so sure about Starletta."

"She don't look worried to me."

"She gettin too full a this Jim Crow."

"How much is too full?"

146

"Remember the promise I told you Starletta and me made to each other?"

"What about it?"

"I got this feeling she gonna go back on her word cause a him."

"So what if she do? Starletta's not gonna quit the show. She ain't the settlin down type."

"You don't get it! Starletta's my twin sister. We got somethin that's special. But if she breaks her promise … Forget it! You don't understand!"

Charmaine raised her hand and ran her finger along Violet's jaw.

"I think I'm a take my 'don't understandin self' on across the room" she said, and moved off among the other guests.

Violet opened her mouth to call out to Charmaine but lost the words when her eyes picked up Starletta and Jim again on the other side of the room. She took another sip of her drink and her eyes watered as the liquor kicked in again.

"That's a good sign," a voice said. "If you can cry, then you always be able to laugh."

It was Jubilee. Violet couldn't stand him, which meant he was on her list of people to coattail for some part of the evening.

"You must cry by the barrelful, much grinning as you do."

"Grinnin ain't the same as laughin," Jubilee said.

"What's the difference?"

"Grinnin ain't always funny. And I don't laugh that much."

"Why not? Can't find nobody around as funny as you?" Violet asked.

"Naw. That ain't it. It's just that what's funny to me ain't always safe to laugh at."

"What about when people are laughing at you?"

"As long as I'm on stage, I ain't got nothin to worry bout."

"Talking to you is like trying to walk through a wall."

Jubilee smiled, but Violet didn't smile back.

"See! I smiled. You didn't," he said. "You can never figure how

147

somebody's gonna act when they hear something they think is funny, even if they the ones that said it."

Violet felt the same shiver wash over her that followed the taste of the pot liquor.

"Starletta and I are looking for someone to do the audience warm-up with one of us at the beginning of every show. Both people talk lowdown and ugly to one another; so if anybody comes to the show ornery and mean, we let off some steam. That way they won't ruin the show by letting off some a their own on us."

"I'll do it," Jubilee said. "Long as I get to do it with you....You know, I was wrong before when I said you were cryin. You probably ain't never cried to keep from laughin a day in your life."

Heat rushed through Violet's face, and she was glad there was a way for her to show her dislike for Jubilee as a regular part of the show.

Charmaine was watching the woman everyone now called "Sweet Knees Louise." There was something about her that Charmaine couldn't quite figure out. She didn't mingle and seemed content to sit, taking in everything with a nervous flickering of her eyes. But it wasn't just curiosity; it seemed more like the need to fill another kind of thirst. Maybe she wasn't used to being around so many people. Whatever it was, Sweet Knees looked lost and out of place. Charmaine licked her teeth as she watched the pawlike smallness of Sweet Knees's hands and the trembling in her lips that looked like she was about to break down and cry.

"What's a matter, honey? Homesick?" she said, squeezing onto the sofa next to Sweet Knees.

"No! Why you say that?"

"Where you from?" Charmaine whispered.

"Kentucky."

"Your people still alive?"

"My mama ain't. And I don't know about my daddy cause I

never got to know him."

"Was your daddy the one that was white?"

Sweet Knees looked down and nodded her head.

"Lift your head up, girl! You ain't the first ever been dipped in the buttermilk."

"I feel a little out a place."

"Why? Cause a this?" Charmaine asked, grabbing the flesh on Sweet Knees's arm between her fingers. "Look at me! There ain't that much difference between us. You can't let lookin like you do make you start actin like you look. You wasn't picked for the show cause a that. You in it cause you can cut it on your feet."

Sweet Knees stared at Charmaine, her face trembling with fear. What was wrong with this child anyway, Charmaine thought. Didn't her mama or somebody ever tell her anything when she was a girl?

Jim had never seen anything quite like the excitement on opening night. They came from all over the St. Louis area and as far away as Kentucky and Illinois. People walked into the theater arguing over what they'd only heard about. When the curtain went up, the entire cast came on stage. The audience was quiet, not knowing what to make of the tossing together of all these different people. Starletta and Violet stepped out in front of the rest of the cast.

"I'm Starletta Featherstone. And this is my sister, Violet," she said, turning her head in Violet's direction. "From where you sit, we may look mixed up. But from where we stand, the whole country's been in a stew. And what we're gonna try to do is make it tasty. So will you all please rise!"

The audience got to its feet slowly, not liking being told what to do. Then Sorrow and Which-Away stepped forward. Which-Away squatted and bent her head into the folds of her dress. Her body made the shape of an upside down bowl as Sorrow started to sing.

> Mine eyes have seen the glory of the land of cotton/Old times there are not forgotten/Look a-way, Look a-way, Look a-way to the coming of the Lord/He has trampled through the vineyards where I wish I was in Dixie/Hooray, Hooray/In Dixie Land he has loosed the fateful lightning of his terrible swift sword/Away down South in Dixie/His truth is marching on.

The audience sang along with the parts of the song they felt closest to during the war. But Sorrow kept going back and forth between the two until they both sounded like one song. And while Sorrow banged the words of "The Battle Hymn of the

Republic" and "Dixie" together, Which-Away lifted her head out of her dress. She grabbed handfuls of her body and acted like she was throwing herself away. Then she made believe she was picking up what she'd just thrown away and stuffed it back into herself.

When Sorrow finished singing, the audience clapped but they didn't know what to make of what they'd just seen. They didn't get any time to think about it because Jubilee and Violet came on stage in black face, dressed like field hands.

"Listening to both them songs at the same time sounds like you when you run your mouth!" Jubilee said.

"That must a really surprised you, since you only used to the sound of your own voice," Violet said, coming back at him.

"You ain't never complained before."

"I do but you never listen."

"This ain't gettin us nowhere," Jubilee said.

"It is for you, cause you ain't never been anyplace but 'nowhere'!"

"If nowhere is my address, then it must be your name."

"Since we're on the subject," Violet said, "somebody asked me who you were the other day; and I told them you were nobody!"

By the end of the skit, their mouthing off at each other rattled the funnybones of the audience and wrung out any anger that anyone had when they walked in.

This show opener was followed by "The Blunder Brothers," a swashbuckling yarn about twin brothers, played in black face by Starletta and Violet. The two brothers were opposites: Starletta was Evil-Abel and Violet was Virtue-Allen. Jubilee, Two-Faced, and Trash played the villains who fought with the twin brothers for the affections of the dark damsel, played by Two-Faced on the backside of his head.

The play kept the audience howling through all the clumsy sword and word play, bungling by characters, unexpected shifts in plot, and its rousing last scene when Virtue-Allen gets his revenge for the murder of twin brother Evil-Abel by killing Two-

Faced's villain with a blunderbuss, then turning him around to kiss the dark damsel in distress on the other side of his head.

Just before the show ended with the dance fest between Jim and Sweet Knees, a cry went up in the balcony, followed by a terrible crash on the ground floor, and screams that echoed to the ceiling. There was confusion everywhere, and people kept yelling out if there was a doctor in the house. One was finally found, and he tended to a man who'd fallen from the balcony. No one in the cast was close enough to get a good look at him. It wasn't until he was carried out on a stretcher that Jim, who'd gotten closer, saw that the man sitting up, waving, and nodding his head to the audience, was the same man who'd jumped off the balcony during the auditions. All Jim could do was shake his head at this fool who was getting more applause than anyone else in the whole show.

Whether the newspapers liked what they saw or not, none of them could ignore the something different that had arrived on the scene with the Featherstone Sisters Traveling Theatre. The papers said it was a show that had something for everyone, a lot of it surprising, and some of it that nobody wanted. One of the surprises was the death-defying leap from the balcony by a white man who, some believed, had been put up to it by the Featherstone Sisters as a publicity stunt. What wasn't surprising was the news that many in the opening night audience weren't pleased that Jim showed his face without any cork.

The show played to sold-out houses every night. By the time their run in St. Louis came to an end, they were booked in five states. The night of their last performance, Charmaine threw a party for the cast. The guests included the low and the not so low from the black side of town. Even some of St. Louis's leading white citizens couldn't pass up the chance to be in the company of the Featherstone Sisters and their motley crew of actors.

Charmaine's parlor and dining room were packed tighter

than a jack-in-the-box. Jim was standing alongside Sweet Knees, whose face was closed like a fist. Jim didn't know what to make of her or why he didn't have much feeling for her as a dancer.

"You never use black face, Mister Crow?" someone asked.

"Never."

"Why not? It comes off, don't it?"

"That's right. But I don't like nothin gettin in the way of the skin that don't come off."

"What about you, Miss Sweet Knees?" a woman asked. "You go along with what Mister Crow said?"

"If it's good for him, I gotta go along with it."

"What about what's good for you?"

"I'm worse off when I stop pretendin than when I'm not."

Jim stared at Sweet Knees and remembered the times when Tom Rice had forgotten to wipe the black face off.

"There she is!" a woman yelled. "The one called Sorrow!"

The crowd that was pressed in around Jim and Sweet Knees broke up and pushed in the direction of Sorrow. This had never happened to Jim before: having people up and leave him to talk to somebody else. Jim looked around, but Sweet Knees was already swallowed up in some other part of the room.

Jim was standing by himself in a crowded room. It wasn't a good feeling. He moved his way over where people were talking to Sorrow. Like the sound of her name, she was very long in the body. And Jim could hear what everybody was calling her "Talk Song."

"The things people say comes before/doing what they say hurts you more./So instead saying something that'll sting/I get it all said when I sing."

"So you think if people sing instead of talk, that'll change what they do?" a man asked.

"More words have led to war/than songs have led to wrong."

"What about them songs in the show? Now tell me 'The Battle Hymn of the Republic' and 'Dixie' didn't have nothin to do with war!"

"Those songs came after the fighting began./When man already had the battle well in hand."

"This woman's gettin me dizzy with all this rhymin!"

"I rather be dizzy from singing in rhymes/than to die from words that lead to a crime."

"I don't know 'bout any of these folks," a woman said. "This one sings but don't talk. And the one over there don't do either."

Jim turned around to see who the woman was talking about. He saw Starletta and Which-Away in a corner, with an audience of their own.

"If you want to know something about her, talk to her, not to me," Starletta said.

"How come you can't talk?" a woman asked.

Which-Away touched a finger to her mouth and shrugged. Jim moved closer and saw her sun-baked face with features of the jaw, nose, and mouth that favored a woman and a man. Everything about her seemed to be going in more than one direction. Her pitch-black hair was parted up the middle of her head and fell over both shoulders. Even the arms and legs of her buckskins looked like they were stitched together from different animal hides.

"You got any kinfolk? Where'd you come from?"

Which-Away shook her head to the first question, and then pointed her finger up, down, to the right, and to the left.

"Guess that explains how she got her name."

"But who raised you?" a woman asked.

Which-Away took the woman's hand, pointed to her palm and rubbed it.

"They were white?"

Which-Away nodded.

"They still alive?"

She shook her head.

"I guess it's hard hearin people talk all the time and not be able to do it yourself?"

Which-Away turned her palms up; then she pointed her finger at all the people asking questions, made her hand move like a mouth talking, and yawned.

"Why you wanna be in a show like this for anyway?"

Which-Away's face lit up like a lantern. She pointed to herself and Starletta, spotted Jim and pointed to him, opened her arms like she was trying to put them around something very big, and then brought her hands together and squeezed them. Jim saw Starletta looking at him just when his eyes started to burn. He rubbed them and realized they were filled with tears.

Just before daylight, all the guests ran, staggered, and crawled out of Charmaine's boardinghouse. Anybody watching would've thought they didn't want the daylight to catch them doing things they would only do when it was dark. Violet and Jubilee sat alone in the parlor as a beam of sunlight sliced through the window.

"That was quite a curtain call we put on for the white folks," Violet said.

"Yeah. It was somethin all right. But I wonder if they'd ever pay to see themselves?"

"They don't have to. They got us to do it for them."

"How you think we did last night with Mister Tambo and Mister Bones?" Jubilee asked.

"Not bad. But the more we do it, the better we'll get at it."

"Funny how that is, ain't it?"

"How what is?" Violet asked.

"How you can get good at hurtin people just by workin at it."

"So?"

"It ain't nothin to bother about. Jus' interestin."

"You don't like people much, do you?" Violet asked.

"What do you mean by 'like'?"

"Having someone you can count on, like family."

"I like havin people around. But I don't want em for somethin I ain't never had."

"Well, what's having people around mean if that ain't family?" Violet asked.

"I mean, like an audience."

"What about when you're not on stage?"

"I'm always on stage!" Jubilee said, grinning. "Strikes me, you and Starletta ain't no different. Outside a Starletta, you don't seem to be all that particular about anybody else when you ain't doin a show."

"That's true for me but it ain't the same for Starletta no more."

"If you mean her bein with Jim, I wouldn't worry bout that."

"Why not?"

"Cause the way I see it, it's just the call a nature."

"Speaking of nature," Violet said, "I've been wondering about yours. You don't care much for women, do you?"

"Not in the way you mean. But it looks like you can't make up your mind either way."

"Am I supposed to make up my mind?"

"Course not! I'm just tellin you what I see."

"I see the same thing in you," Violet said. "Maybe that's why we both do better when we're performin. When we watch other people, we're nowhere near as good as when people are watching us."

"So maybe we ought a stick to what we're good at?" Jubilee said.

"But I can't pretend I'm on stage all the time, like you."

"You're better at it than you think, Violet. And if you'll allow me, I'd like to show you one a these days."

Violet's feeling about Jubilee was getting more difficult to figure out. Here was a man who wanted people around all the time, but really didn't care for them. When he looked at her, she could see his hunger. But it wasn't for flesh; it was for play. And whatever Jubilee was playing, he was much better at it than Violet or anybody else.

Violet tried to sleep but was kept awake thinking about Jubilee, her falling-out with Charmaine, and Starletta's blood. Violet turned back the covers, got out of bed, walked out into the hallway to the next room, opened the door, and went straight to the bed, pulling the blankets off of Starletta.

"Violet! What are you doing?"

Violet didn't answer. She pushed her sister out of the bed. Starletta wasn't sure what Violet was doing, so she didn't move. Violet ran her hands over the sheets but didn't find what she was looking for.

"You don't fool me," Violet said. "Where'd you do it? Outside in the underbrush? You ain't never laid down with no man like that before."

"It ain't your business, Violet."

"It is when you giving in to desire without the blood when it's good for him instead of when it's good for you."

"What's best for me with a man don't have to be the same all the time."

"You never let it happen with any man before," Violet said.

"I'm not talking about any man. I'm talking about this man!"

"What's the difference? He's cut from the same rib as the rest."

"The difference, Violet, is that he's the first man we've ever argued about."

"That should tell you something."

"Like what?"

"He's born under a bad sign. Look at what his dancing's done to everybody who's been close to him."

"You can't blame that on his dancing."

"His mama, his daddy, Tom Rice, and Jack Diamond are probably all dead cause a him. The only one who's left is Jubilee. And the only reason for that is—Jubilee's either the devil's messenger or the devil himself!"

"Violet! Listen to you! Listen to you!" Starletta said, shaking her head, pulling Violet to the floor and rocking her in her arms.

"I hear me fine," Violet said. "You the one not listening! The only way for us is to keep the blood between ourselves and men!"

The Featherstone Traveling Theatre was making a name for itself as it moved through Missouri, Kansas, Illinois, Iowa, Indiana, Kentucky, Ohio, and Pennsylvania. Their shows were different from any other on the circuit. Even the members of the company never knew for sure what would happen from one show to the next. One of the surprises they were never ready for was the man who jumped from the balcony. When he recovered from his injuries, he'd turn up in the town where they were playing, and at some point in the show, he'd jump off the balcony with people cheering when he fell. Word got around about this white man who'd slip into a theater and take a flying leap. So whenever the Featherstone Traveling Theatre came to a town, everybody hoped "the jumper," as he was called, would pick their town to bust up his body in.

Even though people couldn't wait to see the shows put on by the Featherstone Sisters, some of the pleasure was taken away as people whose lives were in a rut watched actors making a life out of pretending. Once during a show in Mercer County, Kentucky, none of the antics by anyone in the cast could hold the attention of the audience. After the show, Jim, Jubilee, Two-Faced, and Trash were holding forth around a fire on the outskirts of town where their wagons were camped. They were joking and trading lies with some blacks who'd come to see the show. Their laughter caught the ears of some white men passing by who stopped to stare and then walked over to them.

"What y'all in such a good humor about? Wasn't nothin that funny on stage," a man said, staring at Trash. " 'Specially that nigger's white man."

Trash's long loaf of a face with its gloomy rye bread color didn't flinch except for his heavy eyelids, which lifted slightly like parted lips.

"You know me from somewhere?" he said, stepping clear of the others.

"No. But I heard about jokers like you."

"You ain't heard about me cause I ain't nobody's white man, yours or anybody else's."

"You hear that boys? He say he ain't no white man!" the man said, bending over and laughing.

"I'm glad you havin the laugh you wanted. At least now you can say you got what you come to the show for," Trash said.

"You ain't the one we want to make us laugh. It's him," the man said, looking at Jim.

"I do the best I can," Jim said, shaking his head. "But I guess everybody's funnybone ain't the same."

"Ain't nothin wrong with my funnybone, nigger!" the man said, taking a step forward.

"Come on, Russ! Let it go!" another man said, grabbing his friend's arm.

"Naw! This boy tryin to tell me on the sly that I don't know what's funny!"

"Since he didn't make you laugh, maybe I can do better," Jubilee said.

"It ain't about you doin better. He's the one cheated me and my friends out our money. So he's either gotta make us laugh now or we take our money's worth out his ass!"

"Jubilee! I don't need you gettin in the way," Jim said. "Let them come on and see how much ass they gotta bring to get some a mine!"

Everybody started coming out of their wagons.

"Sir?" Starletta said. "If you and your friends feel you didn't get what you paid for, your money will be refunded to you."

"Not that it's any a your business, but this here boy and me already got an arrangement to set things right. Don't we?"

Jim started to move toward the man. But Jubilee stepped in front of him and shoved Jim so hard he was knocked off his feet.

Jim was so angry he didn't even feel the blow that put him on the seat of his pants. And he would've been back up again, but he was stopped cold by something he'd never seen in Jubilee's face before. It was fear.

"Jim! Please don't get up again....Look. There's no way I'd go up against you when you dancin. But I'm better than you at what you about to get into. Either way, we past havin to prove anything to each other or anybody else. So let me do what I'm good at, like I let you do when you dance."

Jubilee turned around.

"What you fellas don't understand is that part a my job is settlin accounts with folks who ain't satisfied with the show. So I'm the one you need to see to get what you paid for."

Jubilee started massaging his cheeks with his hands; then he opened his mouth with his fingers almost ear to ear. Everyone in the company put their hands over their mouths to keep from laughing at the sight of the bug-eyed white men. Jubilee reached into his pocket, took out two billiard balls and put one into each side of his mouth. Something popped in the men's eyes, and their faces collapsed like all the air was let out of their heads.

"That ain't funny," one of the men said, taking a deep gulp. "That's impossible!"

"Then why they all laughin?" another asked.

"I just don't see what's so funny bout it," the man said, holding his throat like he was about to gag.

"Maybe it's cause a what we been drinkin."

"What's liquor gotta do with laughin?"

Jubilee started belching; and every time he made the sound, the two billiard balls banged together. This was more than any of the men could stand. They started to choke, throwing up their insides. When their guts emptied out, they were in no mood to fight or talk. The men leaned on each other for support and staggered away.

Jubilee took the billiard balls out of his mouth and flashed a grin at Jim.

"Can I get up now?" Jim asked, smiling.

"A course!" Jubilee said, giving Jim a hand and pulling him up.

Jim looked at Jubilee with a face full of much obliged.

"Don't look at me like that," Jubilee said. "Whatever you about to say, I don't wanna hear it....If them peckerwoods could a seen the faces they was makin while they was lookin at me, they would a really had a good laugh."

"They bugged their eyes out so much, I was ready to hire them to play darkies," Starletta said.

"White folks always make the best darkies anyway," Jubilee said.

"If you ask me, I think those white fellas maybe got a point," a man said, who Jubilee had been joking with earlier.

"Oh? What's that?" Jubilee asked.

"I don't think the way you played with them was funny worth a damn. If they wasn't too drunk to see what you was doin, you might not a got away with it."

"But I did."

"Yeah! And if they come to their senses after you leave, we gonna be the ones to suffer."

"Ain't you heard?" Jubilee said. "It's a new day. We ain't gotta bite our tongue around white folks no more."

"I heard that too," the man said. "But that don't cut no fatback with me, cause I still get paid more in orders than I do in money by the same people who used to hold me a slave. That don't sound so new to me....You all put on a good show. But all that cuttin the fool in the street and actin free and easy with the white folks ain't gonna do nothing but get some of us hung from one a them poplar trees like the two colored fellas lynched right here in Mercer County last year."

"You ain't gotta stay," Jubilee said.

"You know some place any different?"

"You ever lived anywhere else?"

"Only when I'm asleep."

"So the only thing you know for sure is—nothin ain't changed by you stayin here."

"That's easy for you to say."

"It ain't no easier than you stickin with one thing cause you ain't never done nothin else!" Jubilee said.

"Whatever I'm used to ain't gonna do nobody no harm cept me. But you folks are doin things gonna set us back twenty years."

"You mean stuff like this," Two-Faced said, stepping into the glow from the fire. He hadn't wiped off the white face on the back of his head and his pants and jacket were still on backwards. He turned around; and with his back to everyone, he started singing and doing a dance.

> A little old man was ridin by
> His horse was trying to kick a fly
> He lifted his leg towards the South
> An' sent it bang! in the old man's mouth!

Two-Faced's kick into the back of his own head had everybody coughing up laughter that went on into the night in fits and starts.

The Featherstone Traveling Theatre went on showing itself off in front of standing-room crowds. But word started getting around that the Featherstone Sisters and their band of actors were uppity. The only thing Starletta and Violet said about the rumor of their 'uppitizing' ways was that they wished they'd thought up the word themselves.

The shows still opened with Violet and Jubilee trading insults between them. This was followed by a play or skit that poked fun at some event which had a choke-hold on the nation's attention. At the time, the country was all eyes and ears about what blacks were up to since they'd started living more in the here-and-now instead of the hereafter.

So Violet and Starletta wrote a play called "OH SAY, CAN YOU SEE" where Sorrow came on stage and started singing the "Battle Hymn of the Republic" and "Dixie" all at once. Ropes were dropped from the ceiling and some of the cast started climbing down. They were dressed in white and talked to each other about heaven not being all it was cracked up to be and wanting to get back to the here-and-now. The rest of the cast didn't wait to climb down from the hereafter, but started jumping out of it instead.

Once everybody hit the ground, they didn't get very far. Every time they tried to move, they stayed stuck in the same spot. Even when they talked, they kept saying the same thing over and over again. Nobody could figure out what was wrong, so Starletta got the audience to quit laughing long enough to ask them what the trouble was.

"Is this the here-and-now we heard so much about?" Starletta hollered out.

"Yeah!" someone yelled back. "You stuck in the part they call the by-and-by!"

The laughter came tumbling down on the stage. And the audience cheered as the dancing of Jim and Sweet Knees and the singing of Sorrow pulled some people out of the rut they were in. Then Which-Away tied a sash that was almost as long as the stage around her waist. She made a circle with her arms. And one by one, the people who weren't stuck anymore stepped through and crawled underneath the sash, like it was a tunnel leading them to another part of the here-and-now. When the curtain came down at the end of the play, Jim, Sweet Knees, and Sorrow were still trying to dance and sing the rest of the people out of the by-and-by and into the tunnel of the here-and-now that Which-Away made with her arms.

There were some people in the audience who were so dizzy from the non-stop action in "OH SAY CAN YOU SEE" that they had to be carried to the lobby and treated by a doctor. Many who saw the play and watched the cast walking the streets, eating a meal, or just talking came away thinking these people were having too good a time. Didn't they know that the country had fallen on hard times? And if they did, they should've known that misery didn't like being in the company of too much fun. Freedom had gone to the heads of these Negro wenches— which was the last place on their bodies it should've gone to. They'd forgotten their place; and if they were allowed to carry on like this for too much longer, there was no telling how many other folks would start forgetting their places too.

Charmaine liked being around people who didn't stay in their place. Show people never stayed put even when they were on stage, which was why she enjoyed their company. Another thing Charmaine liked about actors was the way they could show their insides to people they didn't know. This made her want to know what kind of chances they took offstage—which was how she and Violet became lovers. But when Starletta's blood started running hot over Jim, Violet sank into a foul mood. Nothing Charmaine did seemed to pull Violet out of the low place she was in; so she left her alone.

There were other people that Charmaine found to her liking. But no one stopped her breath like Sweet Knees Louise. Charmaine couldn't believe that this frisky dancing woman was the same person who walked around the rest of the time like she wasn't sure of her next step.

"Where'd you learn to dance like that?" Charmaine asked her soon after their first show had opened.

"My mother."

"Where'd she get it?"

"From her father. He was kind of a roustabout. My mother told me she wanted me to be able to do somethin that could get me out a Kentucky."

"Did you wanna leave as much as your mama wanted you to?"

"Not at first. But after she died, I knew I didn't want the life she had."

"I reckon some man'll be lookin to take up with you before too long?"

"Well, I ain't lookin to take up with none a them."

"Why not?"

"Cause I got things to do. And I don't wanna be slowed down."

166

"What you do when you gotta answer nature's call?"

"I can't answer what I can't hear," Sweet Knees said. Charmaine noticed that Sweet Knees's eyes weren't jumping all over the place like they usually did. She was completely still except for breathing, which made the thin collarbone between her shoulders stand out even more. Charmaine was wet with sweat. She wiped some of the moisture from her chest with her fingers and rubbed the sweat under Sweet Knees's nostrils.

"Can you hear that?" Charmaine asked.

Sweet Knees held her elbow in one hand, turned her head to the side, and rested it in the palm of her other hand. They she looked at Charmaine with eyes that spoke as clearly as any words she could've used.

Whether it was by train or in wagons, traveling was getting to be more dangerous. There were always incidents where members of the company were insulted, hit, or beaten. Two young black men in the show were even kidnapped and taken to a labor camp in the deep South. The fun-loving caravan of actors wasn't carefree anymore. Many started to grumble and accused Violet and Starletta of coming up with acts that were stirring up too much trouble. Finally a meeting of the entire company was called in a town they were playing in.

"It's not that I ain't grateful for what you done for me," Two-Faced said, standing up in the boardinghouse parlor. "It's just that some of what we doin is gettin too dangerous!"

Others mumbled and nodded in agreement.

"But it's always been this way," Starletta said. "I can't remember a time when we wasn't getting roughed up for one reason or another."

"There's one big difference."

"What's that?"

"We act up offstage the same way we do onstage, and the white folks don't find that funny."

"So what do you think we ought to do about it?" Violet asked.

"We gotta stop doin the white face, let the white folk in the cast go, and quit all the showin off when we ain't on stage."

"Seem like to me," Trash said, "what you proposin would mean that half a you and all of me would have to go."

"That's a good one, Trash. I like that!" Jubilee said.

"You like it!" Two-Faced said, shaking his head. "This ain't no fuckin audition, Jubilee! We can't keep jumpin out our mouth with stuff that our asses can't stand!"

"I think you do better just speakin for your own ass."

"Hey! That's just what I'm doin," Two-Faced said, "tryin to remind everybody, in case you forgot, that coverin our ass is the first law of nature."

"That depends on your nature, don't it?" Jubilee said, playfully.

"Well, my nature likes it here just fine," Trash said. "But if Starletta and Violet say I got to go, it won't be the first time. That's how I got my name in the first place. I was left in a heap of throwaway when I wasn't much more 'n spit. Somebody found me, kept me for a spell, then passed me on to somebody else till one day I was passed on to myself. That was the day I started to like my name cause I knew I was one piece a Trash I wasn't ever gonna throw away! So whatever you feel you gotta do," he said, looking at Starletta and Violet, "I won't hold it against you. Trash'll be fine."

"Well, if you ask me, we ought a take him up on it," Two-Faced said, looking around the room.

"You ain't in it, Two-Faced," Trash said. "I ain't goin nowhere on your say-so. It's up to Starletta and Violet."

"Well, now! Will you listen to the trash talk white!"

"Two-Faced, you know I don't like white that close to my name. You only one word away from me bein all over you!"

"Stop it! Both of you!" Starletta said. "Let me just say this right now. Far as I'm concerned, nobody gettin let go, unless they wanna go. That goes for Trash, Sorrow, or anybody else."

Starletta looked at Trash and then at Violet.

"I go along with Starletta," Violet said.

The quiet in the room started to stink like the smell of food left out too long. Sorrow started humming, which slowly moved her to a moan and finally a wail. Which-Away walked in front of each person in the room, put her hand over their mouth, cupped her hands over her own mouth, and made sucking sounds. Then she crossed her forearms, making the shape of an X, and covered her mouth with her right hand.

No one knew what to make of what Which-Away had done.

Then Starletta looked over at Jim.

"What about you, Jim?"

He looked back at her, knowing what she was asking him but not sure of what he should say.

"You all know the stories about me. They say I danced folks into freedom that sent many to an early grave. My mama and daddy in two a them graves. But I don't know where neither one of em is laid to rest. If my dancin got people to do somethin that lost my folks their lives, I'm damn sure not gonna say nothin out my mouth that might get some a you into the ground sooner rather than later....You all the only family I got left, and I won't side with nobody that gets us tearin at each other like we doin. Once we start that, it's over. We won't never get our hearts back in the show again. Maybe that's what Sorrow and Which-Away is tryin to tell us."

"Wait a minute!" Jubilee shouted. "I think I got a way for us to keep ourselves out the cemetery and still do a show that's worth doin."

"How's that?" Starletta asked.

"We can do a skit where we do away with the white face along with the frowns, so by the end a the show it looks like we glad instead a mad....First we white-face one side of our faces and black-face the other side. Then we use our fingers to fight with our face over whether its gonna smile or frown. When folks see that, I bet you they'll holler and hoot for more."

The tricky road traveled by Jubilee's words caused a trickle of laughter that spread to everyone in the parlor.

"That way," Jubilee said, "it looks like we gettin rid of somethin, when we really just addin more to what's already there."

"Well, I guess by the looks on your faces, we don't need to vote on whatever Jubilee was trying to say," Starletta said, looking around the room and trying to stop laughing.

"There's one more thing we need to do," Jubilee said, "to make sure everybody understands what I think I was tryin to say."

He took a piece of burnt cork and a can of white face cream out of his pocket. He put them on his face and hands. Then he took off his shoes, pants, and shirt and started unbuttoning the shirt of the person next to him. It didn't take long for everybody to figure out what Jubilee was up to.

Soon everyone was taking off their clothes, putting on someone else's, and smearing white face cream and burnt cork on their bodies. Two-Faced was the only one who didn't join in at all. He started yelling that what Jubilee was doing wasn't going to change anything. But his voice was wiped away in all the cream and cork. While Jim didn't go as far as putting on the cream or charcoal mask, he did join in when everybody started changing into each other's clothes. This went on until everyone was sprawled around the parlor in a get-up belonging to someone else and smeared with charcoal and cream.

Before leaving the parlor, Jim told Which-Away he wanted to talk with her.

"I'm like you," he said, when they were alone. "I was raised by some people who found me. I never knew where I came from before that. You know where you came from?"

Which-Away shook her head but stretched her arm out like an arrow and started pointing in different directions.

"You know what happened to your people?"

She closed her eyes, let her head drop forward like she was asleep, and rubbed the fingers of one hand across the palm of the other.

"They was killed by whites?"

Which-Away nodded her head slowly.

"How'd it happen?"

Which-Away didn't answer but just stared back at Jim like she didn't hear him.

"I know my daddy was lynched but I don't know what happened to my mama. She's just lost," Jim said.

Which-Away shook her head suddenly, grabbed Jim's hand

and pulled him outside. Then she started taking deep breaths, jumping up and down and waving her hands like she was watching something terrible happen.

"What are you trying to tell me?" Jim said. "I don't understand."

But Which-Away went on with what she was doing, not caring if he understood her or not.

As it turned out, the changes Jubilee said they should make in the show kept the lid on a lot of the anger coming from the audience. But when nothing they did worked, they'd get together afterwards, change into each other's costumes, and play different parts from the ones they did in the show. This brought everybody closer together, at least for a while.

Sweet Knees's father left her mother soon after she was born. Her mother supported them by taking in clothes to wash. She was not a mean person, just standoffish, without any strong drive to do more than provide for herself and her daughter. Sweet Knees couldn't remember her mother ever holding her after she learned to walk. And she couldn't recall anything that ever gave her mother pleasure. Even when she started showing Sweet Knees how to dance, it seemed more out of sadness than joy. Sweet Knees could only guess about any real desires her mother had, which might have been the reason for her being gone for hours when men sometimes visited their run-down cabin.

What a surprise it was for Sweet Knees when she woke up one morning to find herself excited at being held in her own arms. She'd known what it felt like to be handled and moved around by her mother, but she'd never had anybody touch her to show how they felt about her. It was something Sweet Knees only did for herself until her nostrils were touched by Charmaine's sweaty fingers.

When the company returned to St. Louis, Sweet Knees told all this to Charmaine as well as what Jubilee had done to keep them all together at a moment when they seemed to be coming apart.

"There's something else I wanna tell you," Sweet Knees said, looking at Charmaine across the table where they had just finished eating breakfast.

Charmaine saw a shiver go through Sweet Knees's body and thought she knew what was coming.

"What? That you got no use for men?"

"Why you think I was gonna say that?"

"From what you said it was like for you and your mama, fending for yourselves with your daddy gone, I figured that's how you might feel."

"I have no memory of my father. So it seems like if I had a grudge, it'd be against women, bein the way my mother was. But it don't make much difference to me either way. Most folks don't have much use for themselves, let alone anybody else. I know cause I used to be one of em. At least my mother gave me the one thing she had that I could put to use....But that ain't what I wanna talk about. You know, I never told you the name I had before I came here."

"I like Sweet Knees fine."

"So do I. When that man yelled 'Sweet Knees' at me when I tried out for the show, it made me think that maybe I could really be a different person from the one I was. But there's somethin about who I was that I can't get away from."

"What's that?"

"I'm white."

Charmaine's neck stiffened.

"Since when?" she said, not believing Sweet Knees was serious.

"My mama was white, same as my daddy. And we were dirt poor. I grew up right alongside the colored."

"So how long you been makin believe you colored?"

"I never said I was. But everybody thought so, so I let em go ahead and think it."

"Why?"

"Cause I wanted to be in the show."

"Why you tellin me this now?"

"I don't want you thinkin I'm somethin I'm not."

"Forget what I think. What do you think you are?"

"I'm not colored."

"You can't seem to make up your mind. Can you?"

"What you mean?"

"First you say you're white. They you say you ain't colored, but you don't mind if people think you are. Which way do you want it? Do you want folks to know you white?"

"I don't know."

"So it's all right if nobody knows but me?"

"I guess so."

"Oh! I think you know all right. You just said you did it cause you wanted to dance with this colored-run travelin show. I got no problem with that. Everybody's makin believe about somethin. So you ain't told me nothin I don't already know."

"But you didn't know about ME."

"That don't matter."

"It don't bother you that I'm white?"

"Not as much as it seem to bother you."

"That ain't it!" Sweet Knees said.

"If that ain't it, why you bringin it up?"

"Cause you the only person I ever let get this close. And I don't wanna keep this from you no more."

Later that evening, when they lay braided together in bed, Charmaine wondered why she was so upset by what Sweet Knees had told her. Maybe it was because what Sweet Knees said came as a complete surprise. Charmaine knew there was more to most people than what was there to see. But it was easier to accept that when the person was not in your life. She pressed her face into the strong smell of vinegar at the back of Sweet Knees's neck. Charmaine could understand why Sweet Knees was afraid to tell anyone her secret. She was also afraid to tell hers. Just like it was better for Sweet Knees if everyone else believed she was colored—Charmaine felt it was better for her if Sweet Knees believed there was only one person whose touch could turn her to steam.

Like everyone else, Jim had gotten caught up in the excitement of all the clothes and make-up being passed and smeared around. He remembered Tom Rice's funeral where burnt cork was handed out and smudged on the cheeks and foreheads of mourners to honor the man who spent more time in black face than in his own face. And here was Jubilee mixing up everything they wore, from cork to cream to clothes, so they could save face with one another while still showing their behinds on stage.

What Jubilee had done also made Jim face up to his feelings about Sweet Knees. Over the years, he hadn't met many dancers who could even come close to what he could do. But Sweet Knees's arrival came at a moment when Jim had to accept that he couldn't do what used to come easily. It wasn't anything that anyone else could see. But he could tell. Jim was almost fifty years old and still in very good shape. But in the last few years, he didn't have the stamina to push himself up to the next floor of the unknown where he was as surprised as anyone else at what he could make up on the spot. So instead of risking failure every time he danced, his dancing now had the feel of someone trying not to fail.

When Jim joined the Featherstone Traveling Theatre, Starletta suggested that he and Sweet Knees dance together. But Jim refused. He wasn't sure if it was jealousy or his fear of dancing with a woman who could've passed for white. Whatever it was, he went out of his way to avoid her and never had very much to say to her.

One afternoon Sweet Knees was working out some routines on a butcher block in the back of Charmaine's boardinghouse. Everybody knew she'd been keeping company with Charmaine for some time. And as Jim watched her feet go to town on the butcher block, he wondered if that was something else that bothered him. He didn't think so. After all, Starletta had kept company with women before they met, and for all he knew might still be doing it. But that was something they never talked about.

Starletta wouldn't have stood for it. She told him once that if he met somebody he wanted, he better go after her because that's what she was going to do if it happened to her. The only thing she didn't want either one of them to do was to parade another woman or man in front of each other. If they couldn't keep what they were doing to themselves, then they didn't need to be together anymore.

No. It didn't bother Jim that Sweet Knees and Charmaine were together. He kept watching her and couldn't figure out why she made him feel so uneasy. Then it hit him that he'd never looked straight at her before, or any other woman who looked as white as she did. To look was to touch. And to look like you wanted to touch could get you killed. Jim had to admit that he liked looking at Sweet Knees. But what he liked even more about looking was the feeling that it wasn't a matter of life or death.

Sweet Knees stopped dancing when she saw Jim watching her. She stood still, not knowing what else to do.

"How you?" Jim said.

"I'm fine, Mister Crow. I hope everything goes well by you."

"I was watchin you tote that butcher block out here. It didn't look like it gave you no trouble."

"Not much. My mama took in clothes from around the county when I was a girl. Soon as I was old enough, I helped tote the clothes baskets back and forth. I had to learn to keep up cause she wasn't stoppin."

"Now it looks like everybody gotta keep up with you," Jim said, moving a few steps closer. Sweet Knees squinted into the sun's glare. She shifted her weight to one leg and ran her hands over her arms like she didn't know what to do with them.

"I ain't sure I follow you, Mister Crow."

"Girl! The way you dance, you ain't got to follow nobody!"

"I thank you for that, Mister Crow. I didn't know you felt one way or the other 'bout anything I did."

"No need to thank me, 'specially after the way I been treatin you....Course, you might say I ain't been treatin you at all."

Sweet Knees finally trapped one hand under her armpit and covered the smile on her mouth with the other.

"Mister Crow, I been wantin to tell you for the longest how much it honors me to come out right before you in the show."

"You know, near bout ten years ago I was in a show run by a man named Thomas Rice. I'd been with him fifteen years when he told me not to mister him no more. He was a good man. It just took him a while to get the hang of freedom. I'm still tryin to get the hang of it myself. But I figure I ain't gotta wait fifteen years to tell you not to mister me. Jim'll do fine....Maybe it'll make up some for the way I been actin, if instead a comin out before me, you start comin out with me."

Sweet Knees's mouth hung open.

"Don't just stand there with your jaw dropping," Jim said. "Hit the butcher block! And if you show me somethin you ain't never done before, I'll try'n show you somethin I forgot."

Jim couldn't believe it when Starletta told him they could only make love at a certain time of the month. He understood her reasons. He didn't want to have any children either. But what bothered him was the sight of all that blood. Jim found it diffi-cult to look at blood or bleeding as something natural going on in Starletta's body. When he thought about his own blood, all that came to mind was the night he was cut. But Starletta talked about blood like it was no different from sweat.

They were locked together, shank to hip, and their bodies were juicy from the body blood and honey, making them slip-pery and then sticky after they made love. There was something about being this close that gave Jim a chill. He shivered at the thought of how much Starletta reminded him of his mother. Like Whisper, when Starletta talked, it was like she was thinking out loud. So whatever came out of her mouth was usually what she felt. Jim was used to seeing Starletta flirt with men and women. He could always tell who she was interested in. Her talk got stingy, but her eyes looked greedy. Which was the way she'd acted around Which-Away since the first night the show opened in St. Louis. But it didn't take long for Jim to figure out that no matter who was in Starletta's life, they all had to get in line behind the world she made up in her head.

The morning after Jubilee got everybody to wear each other's clothes and smear their faces, Jim stood in front of the mirror in Starletta's room, looking at the cloth she'd used to wipe the cork off her face.

"Too bad Tom Rice didn't live to see this," he said.

"But you did," she said, standing behind him, watching him

nod at her in the mirror.

"This used to be what helped me when I couldn't make up my mind about somethin," he said, staring at the stain in the cloth. "I knew how I felt about blackin up and everything that was a part of it. But it ain't like that no more."

"You talk like you never had no part in it."

"I didn't!"

"Jim! Even a donkey ain't dumb enough to go for that tale."

"What you mean?"

"It don't matter that you never blacked up. You made a name for yourself from it, same as those of us who used it."

"That ain't the same thing!"

"No it ain't. But that don't mean it didn't leave a smell on you."

"Ain't no smell on me!"

"If there wasn't, baby, you wouldn't be alive; and I wouldn't be bothered with you!"

Jim's hand trembled as he held the stained cloth.

"My daddy never used this but acted like he was blacked-up all his life. He said the way to deal with white folks was show em everything they wanna see except what's on your mind. But they killed him anyway....And when those men got a hold a me, they wiped this all over my face and tried to cut a shit-eatin grin up to here!"

He pointed to his ear. "They didn't cut that far but they left me a face I can't wipe off! And that's the only one I'm ever gonna wear!"

Starletta's eyes had turned into puddles of water.

"Jim. We all hurt when somebody tries to turn us into something that ain't human."

Jim started to say something, but Starletta made a shush sound just like Whisper used to do when he was a child. She reached out and took the stained cloth from him and wiped the palm of her hand with it.

"It's what people do that you need to worry about. Not the

180

things that remind you of what they do. Like this," Starletta said, holding out her blackened hand. Then she lifted her night-gown, put her hand between her legs and showed him the blood.

"Or this," she said and wiped her hand over her face.

"What you …"

Starletta put her fingers up to his mouth. Jim's eyes were like blisters about to burst when Starletta moved close to him and rubbed the scarred side of his face with the hand that was black and bloody. The water broke in his eyes and she held him while his whole body shook without let-up.

When Violet first found out about them, she told herself it didn't matter. After all, she was the one who'd broken it off. But something else nagged at her. Violet kept going back to what she felt every time she saw Charmaine with Sweet Knees. Sometimes a muscle knotted up in her thigh, or a hot flash went through her face, or sweat broke out behind her knees, or she just got a thirst that no amount of water could satisfy. Once after seeing them together, Violet remembered the time Charmaine ran her finger along the side of her jaw. That had been the last time she'd touched her! How she missed Charmaine's hands! Hands that rubbed the gullies between her neck and shoulders, squeezed the muscle just above the heels of her feet, and fin-gered the palms of her hands, the soles of her feet, and the place at the peak of her thighs where the good Lord split her!

Violet returned to the boardinghouse in a bad mood and found Jubilee and Two-Faced sitting in the parlor.

"Here," Jubilee said, handing her a cube of sugar.

"What's this for? I ain't no damn horse!"

"You look like you need somethin sweet in your mouth."

"The taste that's in there now is fine with me."

Jubilee shrugged, opened his mouth, and very slowly put the sugar cube inside.

"What about me?" Two-Faced asked, like he was hurt.

Jubilee took another cube, put it in the cave of Two-Faced's mouth and then wiped his fingers on his own mouth. Violet figured they were playing a game to make her feel better, so she smiled but without much feeling in it.

"That's better," Jubilee said. "Since you don't want no sugar, where you gettin it these days?"

"You ought a stick to show business and stay out of mine."

"With you, it's hard for me to keep track of which is which."

"Well, I guess you two don't have that problem."

"That's the advantage of having two faces on one head," Two-Faced said. "Sometimes my face is all business."

He pulled at the corners of his mouth with his fingers and made a frown.

"But then sometimes I got to do an aboutface cause I know that all my business is show!"

He turned around and put his hands together in the shape of a big smiling mouth on the back of his shaved head. Jubilee clapped his hands and laughed.

"With your two heads and faces and Jubilee's mouth, you two can go a long way," Violet said.

"We already have," Jubilee said. "Two-Faced and me know where the public's tastes run even if they ain't ready to admit it. And they start here."

Jubilee opened his mouth to the fullest, giving Violet a look at the grapefruit pink of his gums, the ivory white of his teeth and the juicy slab of his tongue.

"This is the largest pore in the human body. And mine's larger than most. A lotta things we enjoy in life come from what we put in our mouth. So when people see how much I can get in mine, it stands to reason they gonna wonder what it's like to be inside. But you see, they studyin on the wrong thing. It ain't my mouth that makes me tasty. It's my mind!"

"What you got in your mind that tastes all that good?" Violet said.

"Thoughts!" Jubilee said. "I had em in slavery. And I took em

182

with me when I run off. But it wasn't enough to get out a slavery. I had to get what was in my head out a my mouth and into the world. And I ain't never found a better place to do that than on a stage. But the show don't end for me when the curtain come down. I gotta work my show all the time and in a different way every time. So it don't matter if I'm on stage or keeping company with Two-Faced here, I never do nothin the same way twice. A lotta folks don't like that cause they too used to doin somethin to somebody or havin somethin done to them. But I'm more than that! And I can do more than that! Two-Faced understands—which is good for me and better for him!"

Jubilee stuck his tongue out at Two-Faced, who crumbled into laughter.

"Next to you, John Henry's a spindling boy!" Violet said. "Now I know who put the 'loco' in locomotive!"

She shook her head and all three of them started laughing. But the joyful noises coming out of Violet's mouth made her wonder later how much longer they'd be able to get away with swallowing whatever the white folks forced down their throats, keeping what they could use and spitting the rest back in grins, laughter, and watermelon rinds.

The Featherstone Traveling Theatre kept up its two-faced show, imitating a country that also had two faces when it came to making good on the promises Lincoln made to bind up the nation's wounds after the Civil War. It was a common sight in towns, villages, and cities in Kansas, Missouri, and Illinois to see the daily arrival from the South of horse- and mule-driven wagons filled with blacks with hope squeezed out of their eyes. Many whites, who only knew about blacks from minstrel shows, found it strange living around the blacks who didn't act the same as the ones on stage. This was very confusing and made whites in these Midwestern states very uncomfortable.

Pressure was put on local governments to pass more Jim Crow laws. Curfews started cropping up in many cities, making it unlawful for blacks to be on the streets after ten at night. In other towns, blacks were only allowed to walk on one side of the street. There were also certain sections of town called the Buttermilk Top and the Buttermilk Bottom that were only for whites and blacks. Some storeowners even went so far as to label clothing and other goods for WHITES or COLORED only.

These attempts to keep blacks in their place didn't always work. Many blacks walked on the wrong side of the street, crossed the line dividing the Buttermilk Top from the Buttermilk Bottom, and pitched a fit when a storeowner said they couldn't buy something they wanted that said WHITES ONLY.

As bothersome as these incidents were to whites, nothing was more upsetting than black people laughing out loud. The sound knocked over anything put up to keep blacks out of sight and out of mind. Whites, who were used to laughing at blacks on stage and off, didn't like it when they weren't in on a joke that might've been on them.

Rumor had it that a town meeting was held in a Southern city to figure out what could be done about this. After a lot of talk that left bellies flatter from all the laughter coming out of them, it was decided that whitewashed barrels, marked FOR COLORED, would be placed in certain locations on the street for blacks to use whenever they were overcome by the urge to laugh. It was no surprise that when blacks in the town heard about this law, they laughed before they could find a barrel to stick their heads into.

Laughing barrels caught on in cities all over the South and in places in the Midwest like Jefferson City, Missouri, where Violet and Starletta had booked the show. The story of the laughing barrels was on the front page of many Midwestern newspapers. Just about everybody in the company couldn't wait to get to Jefferson City to see them. But there were some like Jim and Jubilee who weren't as excited as everybody else.

"If we used them barrels in a show, that's one thing. But when white folks expect us to use em for real, that ain't funny in the same way," Jubilee said one evening when they were sitting around the table eating dinner.

"Well, what if we work the laughing barrels into the show?" Starletta asked. "Maybe then, people won't take them so seriously."

"I don't think that'll make any difference," Jim said. "White folks want us to act like we do on stage all the time."

Sorrow started humming and before long the sounds turned into words.

"Before I was singing in rhyme/I waited for menfolk who went off marching in time./I tried to keep things like they was always kept/But nothin stayed put like before the men left./So if folks want us to stay the same no matter what/I hope they don't find out we been foolin 'em with our stuff 'n strut."

"What's all the fuss about?" Violet asked. "If none of us laughs out loud in the street, there won't be a problem."

"I hope you right," Jim said. "But it's their show. And if we don't wanna be in it, we might have to get out a town in a hurry."

"Trash? What you think a these laughing barrels for colored only?" Jubilee asked, trying to lighten up the mood in the room.

Trash was wise to what Jubilee was doing, and his face brightened up like sun-baked corn.

"As you all know, I've seen the inside of a lot a barrels in my time. So I wanna get a good look-see at any barrels that don't have nothin in em but laughs."

"Well, I wanna go see em too," Charmaine said.

Violet looked at Charmaine with eyes that turned to ice picks.

"You never wanted to travel with us before," Violet said. "Why all the interest now?"

"I don't get out a St. Louis that much, but these laughing barrels are something I don't wanna miss."

"What do you think about these FOR COLORED laughing barrels, Sweet Knees?" Violet asked, in a tone that didn't sound like she really wanted an answer.

Sweet Knees met Violet's stare without blinking.

"I don't know what I think about em yet. I have to see em first."

Before Violet could say another word, Starletta kicked her in the leg underneath the table. But Violet didn't pay her sister any mind.

"You don't have to see somethin to think about it. I was wonderin whether you might ever feel the need to stick your head in one of them barrels?"

"I don't laugh all that much."

"I would a thought being around Charmaine would be enough to fill more than one laughing barrel."

"Heifer!" Charmaine said. "If you gonna mention my name in front a me, then talk to me!"

"What's come over you, Charmaine? That fair skin of yours seems to be getting thin."

186

"If you don't get out a my business, I'm gonna get in your face!" Charmaine said, standing up.

"I don't mind. Don't you remember? Gettin in my face used to be your business!"

"Is that what this is all about?"

"No! She's what this is all about!" Violet said, looking at Sweet Knees.

"What about me?" Sweet Knees asked.

"That's what I want to know. There's something about you that ain't right."

"She's with me and you ain't!" Charmaine said.

"I can fix that!" Violet said, jumping up and reaching across the table for Charmaine with one arm and Sweet Knees with the other.

People at the table either watched or tried to pull Violet, Charmaine, and Sweet Knees apart. But Which-Away was standing, breathing heavily with her mouth open. She started making noises that sounded like they were coming from a place deep inside her. She pulled at people like she wanted to put her arms around them. Everyone stopped and stared at Which-Away, who jerked herself one way and then another like she was no longer skin and bones but was just the breath in her body. Starletta went over to Which-Away, grabbed hold of her, and held her until she was calm—except for her eyes, which were wild with fear.

"What is it, Which-Away?" Starletta asked. "What are you trying to tell us?"

"Don't you get it!" Jubilee said. "She was showin us what happens when we fight among ourselves. Ain't that right, Which-Away?"

Which-Away said nothing and looked like her mind was off visiting somewhere else. Maybe Jubilee was right, Jim thought. But he couldn't stop thinking about the morning Which-Away pulled him out into the street and worked herself into a frazzle. And there was the look on her face that was like somebody staring at something they couldn't see but knew was there.

The company arrived in Jefferson City very late, but everyone was up first thing the next morning. They left the boarding-house in the Buttermilk Bottom and as usual turned the heads of a lot of people they passed on the road. When they reached the town square, it was jammed with folks. Above the crowd was a statue of a soldier on horseback. The soldier was pulling on the reins of his bronze horse that was reared up on its hind legs. When some people started moving away, everybody from the Featherstone Traveling Theatre was able to get a closer look.

The laughing barrels were about four feet high and about the same distance around. They were lined up in a row. And every-one who walked by them looked inside the way someone would if they were passing a coffin.

"It feels like somebody died," Jim said.

"Somebody will if enough of us don't laugh in these barrels," Jubilee said.

"Why all these colored folks look so down in the mouth?"

"They probably don't wanna show no teeth, figurin the white folks'll use any excuse to get one of em to stick their heads in."

"If this is what laughing barrels are doing to everybody," Starletta said, "folks'll be beating down the doors to get to see our show!"

Starletta was right! The show was better than ever, and the audience went wild. Violet and Jubilee made their mean-bladed words cut even deeper into each other. Starletta played so many parts, all anyone could do was shake their head when they found out who was underneath all the changes she was going through. Jim and Sweet Knees were so fast-footed that even people with the quickest eyes couldn't catch all that they saw. Jubilee, Two-

Faced, and Trash cut the fool so good nobody could figure out how they were going to slice the next piece of fun. The show ended with Sorrow's voice making Which-Away act like she was breaking into pieces; then she put herself back together again, but with all the cracks showing.

The cast came back on stage to take their bows and started bumping into each other every time one of them bent over. Two actors came on stage from different directions. They both had a whitewashed laughing barrel. Sorrow got into the barrel at her end of the stage and Which-Away got into the one at hers. They were rolled off by the next cast member in line. When the empty barrel was rolled back out, the next person got in and was rolled offstage. This went on until no one was left.

It didn't seem to make no nevermind to anybody coming out of the theater that whites and blacks were buckling in at the waist with laughter right alongside each other and weren't that far from the laughing barrels.

Starletta always looked in on Violet at the end of every show. Things hadn't been right between them since that morning Violet had busted into Starletta's bedroom.

"How you doing?" Starletta asked, sticking her head into the doorway of Violet's dressing room.

"I'm all right."

"I been kind a worried about you after what happened between you and Charmaine," Starletta said.

"You don't need to worry cause there ain't nothin happening between us anymore."

"Is there anybody else? I mean someone special."

"No. You the only one who was ever special."

"What do you mean was? We still sisters," Starletta said. "That ain't changed."

"Yeah. We still sisters. But not like we were before him."

"Violet. Everything you said was gonna happen, didn't. I didn't quit the show, and I didn't have no children."

"Starletta, it was never about Jim or any of the rest of it. It was about you. You were more important than anything else in my life. Matter a fact, you were my life. And when you wanted to fill up a part a yourself with him, there wasn't enough room for me anymore."

"There was room for you, Violet! There was always room!"

"But not enough. It's not your fault. It just wasn't enough."

"So what now?" Starletta asked.

"When I'm not on stage, I gotta find a way to make myself up out a me, instead of out a you, Charmaine, or anybody else."

Starletta moved over to Violet and put her arms around her.

"Is there anything I can do?" she asked.

"You just did," Violet said.

Jim saw Jubilee standing in the wings of the stage just as he was leaving the theater.

"You goin back to the house?" Jim asked.

"No, I'm a stick around for a bit."

"Looks like we had em over a barrel tonight."

"Yeah, I just hope we can stay in our barrels and keep out a theirs."

"What's the matter, Jube? I ain't never seen you this worried before."

"Oh, I'm all right. It's just that sometimes I don't want the show to end. It don't happen that much. But tonight was one a those times. When everything goes as right as it did tonight, it ain't no fun after it's over."

"You sure you don't want me to wait on you?"

"Naw. Go 'head. I'll be along in a while."

Jim stared at Jubilee.

"What's the matter with you?" Jubilee asked.

"I was just thinkin. It's just you and me left from the old days in New York."

"Man! If you gonna start gettin all weepy and whatnot, you need to take that shit on away from me!"

The streets were just about empty when Jubilee walked past the town square. A white man was leaning against one of the laughing barrels. His body was shaking like he was cold. When Jubilee got closer, he could tell it was laughter that was making the man shake. He looked at Jubilee and started laughing even harder.

"You the one they call Jubilee? Ain't you?" the man asked, trying to get himself to calm down.

"That's me!"

"When I heard about these barrels, I just had to see em for myself."

"You from around here?" Jubilee asked.

"I'm from around a lot a places. Mostly St. Louis."

"How'd you get here?"

"Walked most of it....You don't remember me? Do you?"

"Can't say as I do."

The man walked with a limp, and his left arm was crooked. He started climbing up the statue and slipped and slid around on it like it'd been greased with butter. Three men stopped to watch and grinned at each other. When the man finally got to the top of the statue, he sat with his legs straddling the shoulders of the bronze soldier and looked down at Jubilee.

"You still don't know me?"

" 'Fraid not," Jubilee said.

And as soon as he'd said those words, the man leaned forward and fell off the statue and crashed into the side of one of the laughing barrels.

"You 'member me?" the man said.

And then it all came back to Jubilee. He was the same one who used to jump off the balcony in the early days of the show. The man hadn't crashed any of their shows since a real nasty fall some years back had left him pretty broken up.

"You've come down in the world since you used do this from way up in the balcony," Jubilee said.

191

"After that last bad fall, I had to cut down on how far I was fallin, otherwise the only fallin I was gonna be doin was into the ground."

Jubilee laughed and heard more laughing behind him. He turned around and saw three men walking toward him from across the street.

"Well, I guess I got to see just about everything I come for. Course, there's one other thing," the jumper man said, rapping his knuckles against the barrel. "Could you show me how you do it?"

"Show's over," Jubilee said.

"Not if you laugh like you just did, and don't let it out in here," the man said, pointing into the barrel.

"I did it in the show already."

"Could you just do it one more time?"

"Yeah! Do it one more time!" one of the men said who'd walked over from across the street.

"What you waitin for?"

"I'm waitin for somethin to laugh at," Jubilee said.

"Well, we can't wait. So get your head in that barrel."

"There ain't no need to make a big to-do about this," the man who'd jumped off the statue said. "It don't make no difference to me one way or the other."

"You just relax, old-timer," another man said. "You been actin like a white man up until now. So, we'll take over from here."

He looked at Jubilee and pointed to the closest laughing barrel. Jubilee nodded, bent over, stuck his head in, and laughed. While Jubilee had his back turned, the man came up behind him, kicked him in the behind, and fell on the ground, hollering and holding his foot.

"What the fuck's your ass made out of? Rocks?"

"Billiard balls," Jubilee said, taking two out of his back pocket.

"What the fuck you grinnin at, nigger? You broke my foot!"

"Lemme take a look at those," one of the other men said.

Jubilee handed them to the man who held on in each hand

192

before giving one to his friend.

"Too bad you did that!" he said and smashed Jubilee in the mouth with the billiard ball.

The blow made everything in Jubilee's face go numb. He had no feeling in his lips, tongue, and gums. He tried spitting. And when he blew into his hand, blood and teeth came out.

"I ain't never seen the face you makin now before," the man said.

For someone who liked making faces as much as Jubilee, this should've been good news. But he knew the new face that had just smashed the old one would be the last he would ever make. And when the blood coming out of his mouth got into his eyes, the only thing he could see was red!

Jubilee charged the two men, using his hands for eyes; when he got hold of them, he smashed their heads together, and then butted them with his own head again and again and again. The third man who couldn't get up because of his foot never made a sound as Jubilee kept butting the heads of his friends. When Jubilee finally went over to him, he still didn't say anything. Jubilee bent down, put his hands on both sides of the man's fright-filled face and moved close enough so their foreheads touched. The man started to whimper like a dog just before Jubilee raised his head and butted him, crushing the nose bone between his eyes.

Jubilee stuffed their bodies into the laughing barrels marked FOR COLORED. He looked around and saw that the man who'd jumped off the statue had climbed back up and had his arms locked around the head of the bronze soldier. It didn't look like he was thinking about jumping or even falling off. Jubilee wanted to laugh, but the only thing that came out was a cough filled with blood and more broken teeth. And if Jubilee couldn't laugh, he couldn't live. And if he couldn't live, the only thing left to do was to run.

Early morning risers had a good laugh when they saw the man with his arms wrapped around the neck of the statue in the Jefferson City town square. People who passed by waved at the man, but he didn't pay them any attention. Nobody thought anything of it until a woman screamed when she saw a bloody hand reach out of the barrel and grab hold of the edge. When the sheriff arrived, two of the men were dead and the third was not far from it. It took four men to pry the man loose from the statue. He was in shock and couldn't speak when the sheriff asked him questions. But before the third man died, he said the words: "Nigger minstrel!"

The members of the Featherstone Traveling Theatre were roused out of their beds by the sheriff and his deputies. Right behind them was a mob that had dogged their heels all the way from town. The whole company stood in their nightgowns and long underwear in one long line in front of the boardinghouse. Jim watched the men with badges pinned to their coats holding back the crowd. The sheriff looked at all the actors one by one as he pushed the mustache smothering his lip out of the corner of his mouth.

"I ain't got much time," he said. "And if you don't give me the right answers, you gonna have even less time than I got."

"What's the problem, sheriff?" Starletta asked.

"Lynch the lot a them blubber-lipped gorillas!" someone shouted.

"Hold on!" another yelled. "Some of em look like they got the same pedigree we got!"

"So what! They all fuckin freaks!"

"Three white men was beat to death last night," the sheriff said. "And the dyin words of one of em was that a colored minstrel done it....Is this all your people?"

Everybody jerked their heads around, and it didn't take long to figure out who was missing.

"It's hard to tell right off, sheriff," Starletta said.

194

"Well, it ain't gonna be hard at all for these folks behind me. They just as soon lynch all a you as one."

"If you don't tell him, Starletta, I'm gonna," Two-Faced said.

"You shut your mouth!" Jim hollered.

"Don't you get it? Why you think he run off? He don't expect us to get ourselves killed on his account. And I ain't about to!"

"I can't believe you! He's your friend!" Violet said.

"Yeah! He's my friend. But he's gone and we ain't! I ain't said nothin the rest a you don't feel. You just don't wanna admit it!"

No one spoke right away, which was all it took for them to realize there was something to what Two-Faced said.

"Well, Two-Faced, it looks like you saved your real face for last," Trash said.

"Any face I got is better than the only face you ever gonna have, White Trash!"

Trash charged into Two-Faced, and the rest of the company tried to pull them apart; but all the cussing and body-slamming got them fighting among themselves. The crowd started to cheer and clap their hands like they were watching a show.

Then Sorrow's voice made a small hole in the ruckus that got larger and larger until it was a scream with hurt burning around the edges. By the time the scream turned into words, the fighting had just about stopped.

"We have to stop this/ Before there's nothin left of us!/ Nothin left of us!/ Left of us!/ Of us!/ Us!"

"I need a name," the sheriff said.

Two-Faced got to his feet.

"He's the one called Jubilee."

"I'm a do my best to convince these folks to make do with just one a you," the sheriff said. "But I can't make no promises. So if I was you, I wouldn't let another day catch me in Jefferson City."

As soon as the sheriff walked over to the crowd that was still being held back by his deputies, Jim turned to Two-Faced and punched him in the face. Two-Faced looked up at Jim from the ground but didn't get up.

"You think cold-cockin me makes you better than me. Well, it don't. You hit me cause deep down you wanted to tell the sheriff just like I did. But you ain't got the stomach to come out your mouth like that. You might have some a these folks fooled. But you ain't fooled me!"

Jim said nothing and walked slowly back to the house with everyone else. Starletta watched the cursing, blood-hungry crowd follow the sheriff away from the Buttermilk Bottom. Then she turned around to the hunched-over and scared members of her traveling show that had come to a screeching halt.

By nightfall, there was still no sign of Jubilee. Many from the mob returned to the colored boardinghouse to find that the Featherstone Traveling Theatre was gone. Three men were told to follow their wagons just in case Jubilee tried to catch up with them on the road. Starletta and Violet kept the wagons moving all day until they found an out-of-the-way spot to camp for the night. After supper, everyone was pressed in close to the fire.

"Violet and me have talked it over," Starletta said. "And we've decided we can't hold things together anymore. It ain't just because of what happened today. It's been coming since the white folks started hunting down our dreams and dragging them back into slavery. Now they tracking Jubilee. And if they catch him, they still may come after us. Whatever happened last night, we're marked forever by what folks say Jubilee did to those white men. And unless we're gonna become some kind a militia, I don't see how we can keep riskin being shot at or killed everywhere we go. My only regret is—we turned on each other. So when we get back to St. Louis, Violet and I are gonna break up the show before we hurt each other more than we already have."

Jim got up from in front of the fire, reached into his pocket and held up a piece of burnt cork for everyone to see.

"This is for the part a myself that Jubilee and the rest of you helped me to see," he said, and made black streaks all over his face. He passed it to Starletta who did the same, as did Violet, Sweet Knees, Charmaine, Two-Faced, Trash, Sorrow, Which-Away, and everyone else. Jim opened the trunks where they kept their costumes and dumped everything out in a pile near the fire. Everyone reached into the pile and started putting on whatever was pulled out. They spread out in a line in front of the fire and held hands like it was the end of a show and they were about to take their bows. Sorrow started to sing and Which-Away made shapes with her body that looked like the sounds she was hearing. Then Jim felt his mouth opening and he heard himself singing the words to the song he hadn't heard in fifteen years.

> "Are we who we are when we open our eyes?/Is my face myself or just a disguise?/Do we know who's who when our eyes are shut?/When the lids go down, do we know what's what?/In a place called Paducah, a Negro was cut,/And when his rescuers met his attackers,/They was both blacked up./In the muscle and tussle their faces were smeared,/Till no one knew who was to be feared /But they all knew with their eyes open wide,/They were better off not knowing who was on the other side./So this is the story of how faces can fool yuh,/How it's best not to know/Who's who in Paducah."

The three men who tracked them were hiding in the underbrush. They looked at each other as if they couldn't believe what they'd just seen in the glow and shadow of the campfire.

"It ain't just the one we need to get, it's all of em!"

"I ain't never seen such blasphemy!"

"Ain't no doubt about it. These show people is freakish by nature!"

197

When the three men who followed the Featherstone Traveling Theatre got back to Jefferson City, they told a tale that caused as much of a stir as the one that kicked up when the word got out that Jubilee killed the white men found in the laughing barrels. The company was talked about like it was the second coming of Sodom and Gomorrah with male and female going against the Book of Deuteronomy where it said: "The woman shall not wear that which pertaineth unto a man, neither shall a man put on a woman's garment; for all that do so are abomination unto the Lord thy God." If that wasn't sinful enough, the whites and blacks in the show made themselves up to look like each other. They were no better than that savage brute, Jubilee. As a matter of fact, they were worse. They not only carried on their race-mixing and sex-switching among themselves, but the one called Jim Crow sang a song that told how this blasphemy started in a place called Paducah and how they were going to mongrelize the whole country with their foul and filthy ways! When the men were finished, everyone who was listening had broke a sweat that was boiling to a fever pitch. The sheriff and his deputies were out searching for Jubilee. So there was no one around to throw water on what had become a Bible-toting, fire-breathing mob.

After the ceremony in front of the fire, everyone drifted back to their wagons. Jim stayed by the fire, staring into the flames so hard he didn't hear Starletta come up behind him.

"What are you studyin on?" she asked.

"What Two-Faced said about me....He was right."

"So what if he did what we all might a been thinking about doin? We still didn't do it. He did!"

"Jubilee and me go back a long ways. He almost killed me once and then turned around and saved my life. Those two things always been mixed up with everything else I ever felt about him. And it wasn't no different when that sheriff showed up yesterday."

"Jubilee's the best showman I ever saw," Starletta said. "But I never liked him. And that won't change no matter what happens to him. I have to live with that just like you have to live with what was behind you hitting Two-Faced. But I'll tell you one thing. I wouldn't wish on nobody what Two-Faced got to live with, which was why he tried to wish some of it on you!"

"I should a talked to you sooner instead a tryin to think my way out a all this," Jim said.

"Since we on the subject of what you're thinking, what you got in mind to do after we get back to St. Louis?"

"I might head back East."

"Whereabouts?"

"New York, most likely. What about you?"

"I gotta talk it over with Violet. But I figure New York is the place to start putting together another traveling show."

"Ain't you had enough yet?"

"Enough of what? I'm a trouper from blood to bone, just like you. I mean, why else would I go to New York?"

"Yeah. I guess there ain't no other reason to go," Jim said, stung by Starletta's words.

"Nothing's changed between us, Jim. It'll be like it's always been."

"I'm almost fifty, Starletta."

"So?"

"I figure I need to slow down some."

"You know I can't play house."

"You a lot like my mama. She couldn't keep still neither."

"What would you do if I was to keep still?"

"It don't matter what I'd do. It's what you'd do," Jim said.

"I couldn't do it. I been a rambler all my life."

"And I been ramblin too long. Everything I've ever done has been on the move. I feel like I wanna hold on to whatever life I got left in one place."

"So what are you trying to say, Jim?"

"I'm sayin that almost everybody that's ever meant anything to me was snatched out a my life, like that," he said, snapping his fingers. "They was gone before I could miss em. Now that Jubilee's gone, you the only one left for me to miss before I lose you."

"You ain't gonna lose me, unless you try to tie me down so I can only be one thing in one place."

"That's what my mama told my daddy the night before she left him."

"From what you told me, he put her out."

"Same difference."

"Maybe for you but not for her....But anyway, I ain't your mama."

"And I ain't my daddy."

"But you cut from the same stump."

"That mean I'm a wake up one mornin and find you gone too."

"You can't live without losing, Jim. But between living and losing, I'm gonna make you miss me every chance I get."

That first night on the road back to St. Louis, Violet was as surprised as anyone else when Jim used burnt cork for the first time and sang that strange song, "Who's Who In Paducah?" It seemed as if what Jim did freed everybody up from all the arguing over what Two-Faced had done. But they still couldn't shake off how they'd turned on each other and acted just like the mob that was held back by the sheriff's deputies.

Violet saw the light from a kerosene lamp on the other side of the canvas that covered the wagon that Charmaine and Sweet Knees were in. She walked over to the wagon, looked inside, and saw Sweet Knees folding and packing clothes away in a trunk while Charmaine slept.

"Hey Sweet," she said.

Sweet Knees turned around, looked at Violet, and went back to what she was doing.

"Can I come in?"

"Charmaine's asleep," Sweet Knees said coldly.

"I wanna talk to you."

"I don't want no trouble, Violet."

"I didn't come for trouble. Just conversation."

"What do you wanna talk about?"

"I talk better from inside."

"Why? You can't draw as much of a crowd from inside."

When Violet didn't say anything, Sweet Knees didn't push her anger any further.

"Come on in then," she said.

Violet climbed into the wagon. It rocked, and Charmaine moved in her sleep but didn't wake up. Sweet Knees didn't say a word but kept on folding clothes.

"You knew about me and Charmaine, didn't you?" Violet asked.

"She told me."

"What she tell you?"

"You the one wants to talk, Violet."

"It's just that I wanted you to know why I been treating you the way I have. It was just about over between Charmaine and me when you joined the show. In fact, I was the one who broke it off. I know you think I didn't like you cause you were with Charmaine and I wasn't. But the real reason was—I just never figured on you two being together."

"Why not?"

"Charmaine's light and you're damn near white."

"So?"

"It seems like for someone who looked like you and wanted to be part of a colored traveling show that you'd try to fit in by being with someone who's a lot darker."

Sweet Knees laughed out loud and woke up Charmaine who sat up straight when she saw Violet.

"I like to laugh too. What I miss?"

"Violet just told me she never liked me cause I ended up with a woman as light as you and not with someone as dark as her."

"That so?" Charmaine said, staring at Violet. "Well, she don't think that's as funny as you do."

"That's cause she don't know what we know."

"Know what?" Violet said.

"That I'm white," Sweet Knees said.

"Right? Right about what?"

Charmaine started laughing which got Sweet Knees going again herself.

"White!" Sweet Knees said. "I'm white!"

"You mean to tell me, you been passing for colored?"

"I guess I was. But not when I was dancin. Then I was just livin, not passin."

Violet shook her head.

"What's the matter, Violet?" Charmaine said. "You shakin your head the same way white folks did when they found out this travelin show was run by two colored women and when colored men found out you fancied me."

"That ain't what I'm shaking my head about. I don't like being surprised by things that never crossed my mind before."

"I'm the same way," Charmaine said. "But the trick is: after you see what you never thought about, can you take it like you find it?"

On the way back to her wagon, Violet thought about what Charmaine said and remembered some of the skits she and Starletta had cooked up over the years for the show. But once a show was over, she wasn't interested in taking the world outside the theater the way she found it. In fact, Violet would rather have left it alone.

Before getting to the wagon she shared with Starletta, Violet had to pass Jim Crow's, which her sister sometimes stayed in at night. She passed the back of the wagon and saw her sister sleeping alone inside. Violet walked around to the front, climbed up onto the seat, and looked down at Starletta. Strands of gray hair spread on both sides of the part in her thick head of hair. She ran her finger along the line of scalp made by the part. But just when Violet was about to touch Starletta's face, she stopped herself, got down from the wagon, and walked the short distance to her own.

Trash always made sure he was near Sorrow's wagon at night, so he could hear her voice. They'd never really talked, but he never missed a chance to listen to her. Trash stood close to the canvas at the back of the wagon. Sorrow was humming but at times sounded like she was moaning.

"Who's out there?" she sang.

Trash jumped! Then he saw his shadow stretched out behind the wagon from the light of a full moon.

"It's Trash," he said, stepping in front of the opening of the wagon where she could see him.

"What are you doin out there?/ You scared some of the life out a me."

"I'm sorry. I hope you don't get the wrong idea, Mam. I'm not a peeper. I'm a listener."

"I would a thought most everybody in the show be tired a hearin me/ after all this time."

"No way, Miss Sorrow! I ain't had nowhere near enough of all the sounds you can make."

"Thank you, Trash./ It's kind of you to say that./ And you don't need to call me Miss./ Sorrow suits me fine."

"Miss, I mean, Sorrow, I don't wanna pry into things that ain't none a my affair. But there's some things I'd like to ask you."

"Go right ahead./ And if it's something I don't wanna talk about,/ I won't."

"I remember back when everybody was havin their say about whether the show was gettin folks too riled up—you said somethin bout bein in a place where you tried to keep things the same while the menfolk were gone. Just about everywhere I been, there's always folks who wanna get rid a me. Even in this show. So I was wonderin about this place where you tried to hold onto things instead a gettin rid of em."

"My husband and both my sons went to war./But before they left,/they said the war would be over/in time for them to be home for supper./I had supper waiting every evening for two years,/and kept everything just like they left it./But I couldn't keep the world the way they left it./The war found them./And three different times/a Confederate soldier came to tell me a man in my life wasn't coming back./I didn't know what to do/except what I was told to do./But when it hit me that they weren't comin back,/for the first time/I had to ask myself what I was gonna do./I must a sat around without saying a thing for a month./Then one day, I heard someone singing./I didn't know where it was comin from./Then I realized, it was me./I walked away from that house and the slaves that hadn't already run off./I've been talkin like I'm singing a song ever since."

"It ever bother you," Trash said, "that people left you alone cause you didn't talk like regular folks?"

"That's all right with me/cause it was regular folks/who talked with their mouths and not with their hearts/that I wanted to get away from in the first place."

"I hope my regular folks talkin's not botherin you too much?"

"Talkin to you is fine, Trash./It's when people stop talkin/and start doin too much telling/that I can't stand."

"What happened to the rhyme in your words?" Trash asked.

"When I'm alone or feeling relaxed/like I do now,/the rhymes go away."

"The singing ever go away?"

"Ne-verrr!"

Trash didn't say anymore. He just stood there like he was waiting for something. Sorrow knew what it was and started a hum low in her throat that worked its way up through her nostrils and out into the night.

Jim was lying next to Starletta in the wagon listening to Sorrow sing when he heard someone moving around outside. He turned over and looked through the opening in the canvas. Which-Away was stomping her feet and waving her arms. At first Jim thought she was dancing, but the scared look on her face reminded him of something he'd seen her do before. He turned over on his side and watched what looked like steam rising off her clothes. Jim started feeling sweaty from hot air blowing into the wagon from Which-Away's direction. Then their eyes met; and Jim knew what had happened to Which-Away's family at the same time he saw her burst into a flame like the head of a match.

Jim woke up to a blast of heat, Starletta's screams, and the wagon crackling like bacon on a griddle. The hungry flames ate up the canvas. Starletta jumped through a burning gash that gave Jim a second of flame-free space to jump through. But the flames caught hold of the hem of her nightgown and sucked up her body. Jim ran after Starletta as screams came from other burning wagons. She tried to jerk and twist out of her skin that had turned into hot tar. But it was no use. When Jim finally smothered Starletta's body with his own, her burnt flesh hissed and her face was a blister.

Violet jumped clear of her wagon and tried to find Starletta. She saw Jim kneeling down, rocking someone wrapped in a blanket and moaning, "Not gone? Not again! Not gone?"

Violet twisted her mouth into the shape of an open wound but no blood or sounds came out of it. She fell on her knees and scratched and clawed herself with her hands.

A tide of flames blew in on Charmaine and Sweet Knees before they knew it. And for the rest of her life, Sweet Knees remembered three things: Charmaine hip-hugged around her, a breath-stopping shove into her back that sent her flying out of the wagon, and the flames eating up Charmaine's body before she could jump out of the wagon.

No one ever forgot the last time Two-Faced was seen alive. The white face on the back of his head and his turned-around jacket and pants were on fire. He looked like he was running backwards as the flames chased him from face to face.

Sorrow's wagon was set on fire while Trash had gone to help out some of the others. Then he heard her voice. Trash jerked his head around and heard only one word burning alive in Sorrow's scream: "T-R-A-S-H!" By the third time he heard his name, Trash ran straight for the wagon and was inside just as the fire had burned through the canvas.

After the fire burned itself out, those who talked about the fool thing Trash had done said he must've known there was no way to save her. But something snapped inside him when he heard his name come screaming out of the fire. Nobody had ever called his name and made it sound like they really needed him. So he ran to get as close as he could to the need he heard in Sorrow's voice every time she screamed his name. And it didn't matter if he had to go through fire to get there.

Even before the mob put the torch to the first wagon, Which-Away smelled something burning. She wanted to believe it was food. But she knew it was the smell that got into her breath whenever she thought of the night when whites set fire to her tribal camp. When the smell of the memory got so strong that it burned her throat, she started throwing herself around like she was out of her head. And that's all Which-Away remembered until she felt someone shaking her and yelling at her to come to her senses.

When the Jefferson City newspaper printed what had happened, it said the people who followed the traveling show had only gone to do the Lord's work. When the show people heard a voice calling out to them, they hid in their wagons and fired a gunshot when the posse asked if they could look around to make sure Jubilee wasn't there. A man, saying he was a preacher, called out to them and said no one would be hurt if they let them search their wagons. It was quiet for awhile; and then the people in the traveling show set fire to their wagons and tried to run off. But some brush behind the wagons caught fire and everybody was trapped between the two fires. When the blaze finally burned itself out, only nine of the twenty-three members of the Featherstone Traveling Theatre survived. The preacher told the newspaper reporters that the fire might've been a blessing because the sins of everybody who was killed had been burned away.

Jubilee's body was found rotting in the Missouri River. The newspaper said the cause of death was drowning. But some

blacks who saw Jubilee's body didn't believe he'd drowned trying to escape. It turned Jim's guts when he heard a man say
Jubilee's cheeks were puffed up and his head was beaten in so
bad it looked like ground beef. When his mouth was pried open,
they pulled out his tongue, ears, balls, and penis.

There were two other stories going around at the time the
people of Jefferson City were looking for Jubilee. The first was
that the sheriff was gut-shot with his own gun and died some
hours later after losing a lot of blood. The second had to do with
the man sitting on top of the statue in the town square who was
so shocked by what he'd seen that he decided to stay put. And
so, the man, who'd never gotten that much attention for his
great leaps from high places, finally became famous for refusing
to come down to earth. But for the people who knew about him
from before, it seemed like he'd had a lot more fun when he
risked life and limb than he did once he started keeping his distance from the danger he used to love to jump into.

The nine survivors of the fire traveled by wagon with the bodies of their fellow actors to St. Louis. They were met at the outskirts of the city by the sheriff, the mayor, and other city officials
who told them that in the interests of public health and safety
the burials would have to take place immediately. They were
escorted to a deserted section of the bone orchard reserved for
colored. The graves were already dug and the gravediggers were
waiting when they arrived. Nothing was said about Sorrow and
Trash being buried alongside of blacks. A good-sized crowd
looked on as the fourteen coffins were lowered into the ground
and dirt shoveled on top of them. When the gravediggers were
finished, no one left. It was as if the crowd were waiting to see
what the nine surviving members of the Featherstone Traveling
Theatre would do for the ending of their last show.

When Jim, Sweet Knees, Violet, and Which-Away picked up
on why everybody was waiting around, they took handfuls of dirt

from every one of the unmarked graves, mixed them together in a pile and put some in their pockets. They turned to the crowd and took a bow. Sweet Knees started a dance that made her jiggle at every place on her body where there was a joint. Jim did quick leg lifts that slowed down to the point where they looked waterlogged. A heaviness sank into his shoulders, making his back hunched. Then the spring came back into his step and his spine snapped upright.

Jim and Sweet Knees danced from one grave to the next, doing something different on each one. Violet started talking, and Which-Away moved her body in a way that made people feel like they were looking at a picture of every word being said.

"We just can't help ourselves," Violet said, turning her palms up. "Whenever one or more are gathered in our name, we're liable to make a show out of the occasion. I guess it's only fitting that we have our final public performance out here in the bone orchard where all of us end up for our last go-round. I won't speak about the untimely demise of those laid to rest here, since it ain't death that's untimely. It's life! And there's never enough life to figure it all out....None of us ever really knows WHO that person is when we look in the mirror. Even when we're about to do something, it doesn't mean we know what we're doing or the reason why....That's the story we've been putting our heartbeats into all these years. Now the beats from those hearts buried here have stopped. And each of us will have to carry the story around inside us without seeing it brought to life on stage anymore."

Violet signaled Jim, Sweet Knees, and Which-Away to come over to where she was standing. They reached into their pockets, took out the dirt from the fourteen graves, and handed out a little from each to the crowd. Most people put the dirt in their pockets or held it in their hands. Children were the only ones who didn't pocket the dirt or hold onto it. They looked at it and started laughing and throwing it at each other.

After the crowd broke up, Jim, Violet, Sweet Knees, and Which-Away were stretched out on the two graves where

Starletta and Charmaine were buried.

"Where'd all that talk come from? I ain't never heard you do anything like that before," Jim said.

"I ain't never did a show in a graveyard before either," Violet said.

"It reminded me of what you and Jubilee used to do in your Tambo and Bones act."

"Yeah. We double-talked pretty good together."

"What y'all aimin to do now?" Jim asked.

"You asking me or all three of us?" Violet asked.

"I'll start with you."

"What about her?" Violet asked, flicking her eyes at Sweet Knees.

"Talk to me, Violet. Not around me," Sweet Knees said.

"I don't know you that well."

"So what you gonna do, Violet?" Jim asked again.

"Ain't made up my mind yet."

"What about you, Sweet?"

"I think I'm a stay put. Charmaine didn't have no next a kin. So maybe I can keep her place goin for young girls who've left where they're from but don't know where they going."

"What about dancin?" Jim asked.

Sweet Knees shrugged.

"If somethin come up, fine. If it don't, it don't. Thanks to all a you, I don't have to be just one thing no more."

"You one up on us then, ain't you Sweet?" Violet said. "But that's the way it is when you can make your color go both ways."

"What about you, Vi? Which way your color go?"

"Anywhere! Except near you."

"Don't seem to be botherin you now."

"Well, like you, Sweet, I know how to put on an act!"

"Yeah! But there's one act you ain't learned: and that's how to have fun."

"I don't know, Sweet," Jim said. "Sound like Violet havin a pretty good time right now."

"I don't need you to tell me what kind a time I'm havin," Violet said.

"You need somebody to tell you somethin!"

"If I didn't ask for it, I don't need it!"

"Better get a grip on yourself then, Violet. Cause you ain't through gettin a whole lot you ain't never asked for."

"You ain't never lied!" Violet said, nodding her head.

"I remember somethin Charmaine used to say," Sweet Knees said. "There ain't nothin better than havin somethin you don't need!"

They all broke into gut-busting laughter that went on until they were too tuckered out to talk.

"Where you headed, Which-Away?" Jim said, once he got his breath back.

She looked around and pointed at the road leading into St. Louis.

"You think you might wanna help me keep Charmaine's place open for women who've lost their way?" Sweet Knees asked.

Which-Away sat up, pointed at herself, Jim, Violet, and Sweet Knees and then moved her hands out in front of her like she was trying to find her way in the dark.

"I know, Which-Away. You're right."

"If we lost, there's a reason for it," Jim said.

"Like what?" Violet said.

"You see what those children did with the dirt we gave em? They just throwed it away."

"So what!"

"Maybe that's why we don't know where we are? We ain't passed nothin on."

"Don't look at me!" Violet said. "It takes two to make one!"

"Instead a makin a whole new life, maybe we can pass somethin on by helpin folks that's already here?" Sweet Knees said.

"What you talkin about?" Violet asked.

"It's like what I just said to Which-Away. Maybe all of us could stay in St. Louis and run Charmaine's place."

"Listen to you! Charmaine ain't even in the ground good. And you already talkin about takin over her place! Always the wrong people end up surviving!"

"That go for you too, Vi?" Sweet Knees said.

"Course it does! Look at us! If it wasn't for Starletta and Charmaine, none of us, except for Which-Away, could stand to be around each other!"

"Well, I can do my part to fix that," Jim said. "I'm headin for New York soon as I can get myself on a train."

Which-Away shook her head, pointed at him, locked her fingers together, and then tried to show him how hard it was to pull them apart.

"I can't do it, Which-Away," Jim said. "It don't bother me bein lost cause that's where I started out and where I'm gonna end up. It's losing people that I can't take no more. Right before we got burned out, I had a dream about a wild dance you did in front of me one time. When it hit me that your family was killed in a fire, I woke up in another fire....If I go with you to St. Louis, it'd be like holdin all the feelin I got from losin Starletta, Jubilee, Sorrow, Two-Faced, Trash, and all the rest before them. That's too much for me to carry."

"You feel that way too, Vi?" Sweet Knees asked.

"What do you care? Why you all up in my life for anyway?"

"Cause a Charmaine."

"What she got to do with it?"

"She's the one we was both close to. I feel different from Jim. I wanna keep Charmaine near me. But to do that I gotta stay close to what she left behind. And what she left—is us. Jim already said what he's gonna do. And he ain't asked you, me, or Which-Away to go with him. So unless you goin off by yourself, you gotta decide if comin with Which-Away and me is gonna keep you in touch with that part a Charmaine and Starletta that you wanna keep alive."

"The only thing I want is to forget you!" Violet said.

"You can do that if you want. But you can't forget who we got in common."

"Damn, Sweet," Jim said. "Look like you startin to dance again without you even movin your legs!"

And they kept on in that beat—teasing, nudging, and signifying for the rest of the day and into the night until they fell asleep.

The daylight got up underneath Jim's eyelids and woke him up. Violet, Sweet Knees, and Which-Away were gone. He was upset at first that they had left without saying anything, but then felt glad because he didn't have to bother with goodbyes. Jim got up to leave, took a last look at the fourteen graves, and realized that they had left something for him after all. In the dirt covering the graves of Charmaine and Sorrow were a lot of prints of Sweet Knees's feet and Which-Away's hands. He looked around, but there was nothing from Violet. That made him laugh, which was more than enough to remember her by. Jim dug out the dirt from some of the hand- and footprints and put them in his pockets before leaving the bone orchard. As he walked, he wondered what Violet had decided to do. He could've easily found out by stopping by Charmaine's boardinghouse on his way to the train station. But like the funniest shenanigans on stage that left Jim laughing and wondering what would happen next, he decided it would be better to wonder.

Jim figured that a lot of white people must've wanted to get out of St. Louis in a bad way because there were quite a few sitting at the front of the Jim Crow car when he got on. The train hadn't been out of St. Louis more than half an hour before blacks and whites started turning their heads to stare at him. Finally, a black man leaned over who was sitting across the aisle.

"Ain't you one a the folks who was dancing on coffins?"

"That's right."

"You must be Jim Crow then?"

"For as long as I can remember."

"Well, I hope trouble ain't followin you like it did from Jefferson City to St. Louis."

"If there's a point you tryin to make by sayin that, I wish you'd hurry up."

"It's just that some a the rest of us in this Jim Crow car wanna make sure we get to where we goin."

Jim looked around and saw other blacks with their heads turned in his direction.

"You ain't got to worry none. Those white folks killed enough of us to last them for a while."

"You see!" a woman said. "That's the trouble with you showcase niggers. You get so far ahead of yourselves you lose sight of yourself and your people."

"Oh! So now we too far ahead," Jim said. "Just a few years ago colored folks was sayin the minstrels was holdin the race back."

"That's why you need to make sure you don't 'low yourself to get out a touch," another man said.

"The problem is—it's hard to keep in touch with the colored race cause it ain't likely that I'm gonna meet most of em."

"I'm glad you find this funny, Crow," the man said, "cause you gonna laugh yourself right into an early grave."

"Why not? At least that's one place where we don't have to wait for the white folks to go first," Jim said.

"Why don't you niggers put a lid on it!" a white man yelled from the front of the car.

"Why don't you come on back here and put the lid on!" the man said who was talking to Jim.

"What's that?" the white man said, jumping out of his seat.

"You heard him!" a woman said. "This here's the Jim Crow car. We even got the real Jim Crow back here with us. So if you don't like sittin still for what you hearin, you can go on and stand up in the white class car!"

The man who'd jumped up walked toward the back of the car and was followed by two other white men. The rest of the whites turned around and saw black men and women standing up to greet the visitors coming to meet them from the front of the car.

"We ain't gonna stand for no sass from you blacks," the man in front said.

"Looks like to me you already standin for it," Jim said.

The Jim Crow car just about split wide open from the laughter. The people who were standing in the aisle and in front of their seats had to sit down because their sides were hurting so much.

"Who're you?" the white man said, when things had quieted down.

"I'm Jim Crow."

"I saw you in a show once. You wasn't all that funny."

"You ought a talk to the folks back here," Jim said. "They don't like me neither. But that's cause they think I'm too funny."

The man mumbled something under his breath and went back to his seat.

"Well, Crow, looks like you joked us all out a trouble that time," the black man across the aisle said.

"Yeah!" Jim said, shaking his head. "No tellin what I could a done if I hadn't lost touch with the race."

The train crossed the Mississippi River into Illinois and stopped in East St. Louis. Jim decided to walk around and see some of the city before the train left. He found himself following a crowd of people that ended up in a wide open field. Jim walked under a wooden archway that was like the ones in front of plantations. At first he thought it was a state fair until he saw black women wrapped up in aprons and tourniquet-tight head rags leading people toward cabins, hen yards, hay wagons, chickens, and bushes with cotton balls stuck on them.

Jim was pulled along with everybody else and couldn't believe it when he saw black men and women everywhere in overalls and sheet-thin, ankle-length dresses hitting a few licks of work, breaking out into a sweat, a song, and a dance, grabbing watermelons off wheelbarrows, busting them open on rocks, and eating them down to the rind.

Jim felt himself getting weak-kneed when he heard a voice cut through all the noise.

"Ladies and Gentlemen! Welcome to P.T. Barnum's newest extravaganza! Our great nation will soon celebrate its one hundredth birthday, and newspapers, photographs, and telegraph wires have put us in touch with events and people that are thousands of miles away. P.T. Barnum has been part of this march to bring the rest of the world closer to us. And today, Barnum brings you, not a stage show, but the Southland as it really is! And Negroes as they really are! Look around and you'll see them as you've never seen them before—being their real, natural-born selves! Look! There! There! And there! The Contented Slave! The Wretched Freedman! The Comic Negro! The Negro Brute! The Tragic Mulatto! The Local Color Negro! and The Exotic Primitive!"

Jim walked past black women and men who wore tags saying what kind of Negro they were. The more he watched them go about their business, the more they looked like they weren't really there. Jim saw one man wearing a tag that said: THE

LOCAL COLOR NEGRO. He was leaning against a tree with his mouth turned down in a frown. A white man who was wearing a derby, with thick, unruly, wheat-colored hair reaching down the side of his face, broke through a part of the crowd.

"Come on now!" he said to the man leaning against the tree. "Where's the local color?"

"You lookin at it," the man said.

"But you ain't doin nothing."

"Depends on how you look at it."

"You right. It does. And you ain't showin me nothin colorful!"

"I'm colorful enough for me."

"Then you gotta find yourself another plantation!"

"I ain't leavin till I get paid for the time I put in."

"You know the rules. While you on the plantation, everything's normal. It ain't a job. It's for real. So nobody gets paid till the show's over."

"I'll wait."

"Not unless you come up with something better than what you doin now."

"The situation ain't presented itself yet."

"I can see you wearin the wrong tag," the man in the derby said.

He reached in his pocket, pulled out some tags and went through them until he found the one he was looking for.

"Here," he said, tossing it at the man. "This one suits you better. You got a lot more brute in you than local color."

When THE LOCAL COLOR NEGRO didn't pick it up, the man in the derby reached in his pocket and pulled out a whistle.

"Now you actin like the brute you are. So it's only natural for me to call the police."

He blew the whistle and the man ran into the crowd.

The police came from everywhere, swinging their billy clubs at every black man they saw. Screams ripped through the plantation, and the crowd scattered in all directions. Roosters and hens flapped their wings, and feathers sputtered in the air as they took flight.

Jim was grabbed with some other men, handcuffed, and taken to a large tent in another part of the field. The police led them inside where they saw men and women standing with tags around their necks. The tags on the women said: THE NIGRA WENCH and THE HEATHEN CHINEE. And the ones on the men said: THE DUMB SWEDE, THE DRUNKEN MICK, THE TIGHT-FISTED SCOT, THE SHYLOCKING JEW, and THE MURDEROUS PAISAN. There was also a body that was stretched out, face-down on the ground, with a tag on its back that said: THE DEAD INDIAN.

A man dressed in black came into the tent. His hair, handlebar mustache, and eyes were glossy black like a raven's. He whispered to the policemen and then walked over to the tagged and untagged prisoners and looked them over.

"I know all of you are wondering why you were brought here. My name is Hamilton Strong. I'm a photographer and I'm taking pictures for a national 'Rogue's Gallery' so the police can keep track of troublemakers like yourselves who fit the descriptions on the tags that are around your necks."

"I ain't no troublemaker," the man with THE DUMB SWEDE tag said. "They the ones makin the trouble," he said, looking over at the police.

"Even if you didn't do anything this time, all of you are guilty of practicing one or all of the Seven Deadly Sins which are— foolish pride, covetousness, lust, anger, gluttony, envy, and sloth. But that's really not my affair. My only concern is getting your cooperation so I can take my pictures. If any of you refuse, the officers will take you away and bring you back when you're ready to cooperate."

"What makes you think I'm a let you take my picture when I ain't done nothin?" a black man who'd been brought in with Jim said.

"One way or the other your picture's gonna end up in the 'Rogue's Gallery.' It's up to you what kind of shape you want to be in when your picture's taken."

Everyone followed Strong's eyes to the body with THE DEAD INDIAN tag on it.

"So are we all agreed?"

No one said a word.

"Splendid! All right, officers! You can take them outside now."

The police took everybody outside. They even dragged the dead body out. The handcuffs were removed, and those who didn't have a tag were given a long cardboard strip with a string that was tied around their necks. Jim looked at his and read the words THE CONNIVING UNCLE TOM. Strong set up his equipment as Jim and the other rogues watched the last few skirmishes with the police going on in other parts of the field.

The body with THE DEAD INDIAN tag on it was the first picture that was taken. Jim was second in line and waited for Strong to set up again. When he'd adjusted the brass lens cap and the image scope, Strong came out from underneath the black silk cloth attached to the camera.

"You know," he said, "you're part of an historic moment. You will be the first Negro whose picture is taken for the 'Rogue's Gallery.' So you'll be able to say that yours was the first image of your race captured for posterity right before the nation celebrated its one-hundredth birthday. And maybe, if you know you're always gonna be in the 'Rogue's Gallery,' you'll stay out of trouble."

Jim stared at the eye in the center of the camera box as Hamilton Strong disappeared underneath the black silk cloth with only his legs showing behind the tripod. One of the policemen held the pan of flash powder in his hand.

Then a piece of a dance step that Jim had never thought of before exploded like flash powder in his mind. A chill rushed over his flesh. He couldn't wait to try out the new step and share it with all the people in his life whose goodbyes were still not gone.

"All right! Just hold it right there!" Strong said.

Just before the flash powder went p-o-o-f, Hamilton Strong blinked. When Jim was let go by the police, he started whistling and making a big fuss with his feet. Strong smiled as he watched Jim hoofing his way out of sight. He was glad that Crow was in such good spirits over being picked as the first Negro to be in the 'Rogue's Gallery.' But it wasn't until Strong saw the finished picture that he realized THE CONNIVING UNCLE TOM didn't come out the way he wanted because Jim Crow had moved!

03-08-93

WHO'S WHO

W. T. Lhamon Jr.

One way or the other your picture's gonna end up in the "Rogue's Gallery."
It's up to you what kind of shape you want to be in when your picture's taken.

P. T. BARNUM'S PHOTOGRAPHER TO JIM CROW

When all we have is corrupt legends and missing facts, where do we begin? Kneading them into lively sense is Wesley Brown's method. *Darktown Strutters* opens up an emotional accuracy about Americans' mutual history of race. It begins to offset the facts we lack. It copes with the corruption.

Look at the way Brown replays the opening scene of blackface dance, for instance. He riddles our received understanding of racial appropriation, in which whites are supposed to have stolen the gestures and costume of black authenticity. In the opening scene of *Darktown Strutters*, black Jim Crow tells white Tom Rice: "What I did was show you how I do it. I couldn't give you that dance even if I wanted to. Now if you do somethin with what I showed you, that makes it yours. . . . It belongs to you. And that's different from just copyin somebody" (3). Then Jim Crow also shows the dance to his adopted son, Jim Too, a black boy twice removed from sure identity because at age three he was already separated from runaway slave parents. Thus Wesley Brown squares the inaugural fantasy of blackface into two parallel traditions, one black, one white, both transmitting Jim Crow, both

221

related, both constituting the resurgent performance of what still passes for blackness in the regions of its diaspora.

These complications on the simplistic legend of Rice's "copyin somebody" are a welcome revision in themselves. They nudge consensual history toward a pattern more satisfyingly unschematic. Thus Brown's complications are able to help us understand how specific gestures clustered so powerfully around the Jim Crow dance that many whites and blacks agreed that it flagged "blackness" and tried to own it. *Darktown Strutters* makes another story out of the emotional history of these charismatic moves that have troubled us all since the spring of 1830, when "Jump Jim Crow" became America's first rave song and dance. That's when T. D. Rice consolidated the form that has remained at the center of Atlantic popular culture.

In fact, there is nothing factual about Jim Crow and no single moment of appropriation. The real Tom Rice was an important actor and playwright—arguably the most popular, the highest paid, and the most determinative of his era—who did black up from 1830 through the 1850s. But he did not die violently. His will shows that Rice died peacefully, surrounded by his four surviving children in New York City, age fifty-two in 1860, before the outbreak of the Civil War. And the real Rice did not hire a *man* named Jim Crow to dance for him. Instead he hauled into white view a widespread black folk *dance* known as Jim Crow, which he performed himself. This dance, and the song that accompanied it, was about a trickster figure—as real as Brer Rabbit, no more, no less. Thus there was no historical figure named Jim Crow who taught Tom Rice black dance: it was a folk process. And there was no actual Jim Too. These are wholly social constructs, as legendary in reality as in *Darktown Strutters*.

Although T. D. Rice was one of the most traveled men of his era, here and in Europe, he never ran a troupe of strolling players. Contrary to the legends about him, Rice was not Irish and not Catholic. He married in 1837 in London in the Church of England; his New York funeral service was Protestant, as his heirs have remained. There is no more evidence that Tom Rice was gay than that Nat Turner was—which is to say, none at all. That Brown queered Rice may play tit for tat with William Styron's similar move in his novel, *The Confessions of Nat Turner* (1967), set also in 1831, about that other racial revolutionary. Although numerous blackface acts, including some traveling troupes, started circulating around the states about 1840, they were almost never integrated racially or sexually. A prime exception in the case of race is the instance of William Henry Lane, the famous black dancer who performed as Juba. His cameo appearance here catches him on the way to early death in England.

As soon as we catalog central features of *Darktown Strutters* that never happened, however, plausible counter examples crop up. Brown does engage a larger real history that is still strutting. Jim Too's career draws on Juba's. Although Rice never ran a traveling troupe, in his early career, he once (very obscurely, at age twenty-two) did advertise to start a troupe in Kentucky.[1] Brown clearly modeled his character Jubilee on the great postbellum black minstrel Billy Kersands, who was often photographed with billiard balls in his mouth. (That's either Kersands or someone imitating him in Robert Frank's collage album cover for the Rolling Stones' 1972 *Exile on Main Street*.) The violent draft riots in New York City in the middle of both the Civil War and *Darktown Strutters* were horribly real. And when Brown writes about the practice of dancers confining themselves to "butcher blocks," he glosses the way butchers hired black dancers to perform at New York's markets in the early 1800s, confining them to the space of a shingle. Early lithographed song sheet covers show blackface dancers on such boards—from such conventions tap dancing ascended. The novel's Featherstone Sisters' blackface troupe has a loose basis in companies like the Hyers Sisters' company that followed the black theatrical circuit in the late nineteenth century. And, in a once-removed register, Jubilee's violent resentment at southern laughing barrels elaborates stories that Ralph Ellison described in his important essay "An Extravagance of Laughter."

Thus *Darktown Strutters* stirs up what might have happened with what certainly did, in history and criticism. For those who know the form, the brief appearance Brown gives William Henry Lane evokes the way Juba often challenged white dancers, like the quite real John Diamond that *Darktown Strutters* also reincarnates. When whites refused to compete with him, Juba would simply imitate their styles. And then he would imitate himself surpassing his white imitators. This virtuosity inspires *Darktown Strutters,* which continually mimics minstrel models, going them one better, pushing toward the surreal.

You can call Brown's method signifying on an extraliterary genealogy. You can call it a cutting contest between remembered popular forms and vanguard fiction. Whatever you call it, the method levers back into view the downright upsetting spirit of blackface performance. Brown reminds us of the powerful challenges inherent in theatrical spectacles at specific moments since about 1830, when Rice's dancing Jim Crow jump-started what we mean today when we say "popular culture." Wherever Jim Too dances in *Darktown Strutters,* personal trouble occurs—and so do public riots, often enough. This reminds us that there were real reasons why many elites continually scorned blackface performance and why some southern cities outlawed it in the years leading up to the Civil War. This disdain and proscription relate to the later policing of Lenny Bruce, the burning of rock 'n' roll records in the 1950s and '70s, the censoring of Little Richard and jailing of Chuck Berry, the police beating of Miles Davis and outlawing of Thelonious Monk, the delimited frame of the TV camera on Elvis Presley's body, and the censorship of hip hop features in the 1980s and '90s. All these have to do with the trouble that elites feared when popular arts made their concerted turn toward the "low" for inspiration, as they did in blackface performance, rather than chiefly aspiring up the social scale, as earlier popular arts had. All these reasons underscore the observation that Alexis de Tocqueville made during his American visit precisely when Jim Crow's dance was becoming a theatrical fad: "If you want advance knowledge of the literature of a people which is turning toward democracy, pay attention to the theater."[2]

In revisiting the rude origins of American theater, Brown shows that its strata still map the archaeology of democratic cultural development. There are remarkable aspects to Brown's meditations in these old digs. By thinking hard on what was available to him through legend and histories, he conjures striking replicas of details that had gone missing in the secondary sources, or that history had repressed. *Darktown Strutters* thus conveys cultural imagery that once existed before its own incandescence scorched off its traces in cultural memory. Brown's imagination corrects and supplements history by providing a more accurate material unconscious.

When Brown published *Darktown Strutters* in 1994, nowhere in the printed commentary on minstrel theater was there any knowledge of the special figure he shows both Tom Rice's troupe and the Featherstone Sisters enacting. First, Rice:

> "I got a new skit I wanna run by you [Rice tells Jim Too before the Civil War]. . . . *The way it goes is—we'd all be in black face on one side of our face and white on the other.* When we start talkin out of both sides of our faces, you try to figure out who's on your side and who ain't. We keep the audience guessin right along with you until the end when everybody finds out who's who." (66, my emphasis)

This new skit is the play "WHO'S WHO IN PADUCAH?" It becomes Rice's signature piece, its black-and-white faces finally rousing racists in the novel to assassinate the play's author and actor on stage.

Second, the Featherstones, for Brown also insists on this troubling iconography after the war. Toward the end of the Featherstone Sisters' traveling show, when they are already on the run for their guerrilla theater, with southern audiences accusing them of "uppitizing' reality (164), Jubilee reinvents what seems to him a new strategy:

"I think I got a way for us to keep ourselves out the cemetery and still do a show that's worth doin. . . . *First we white-face one side of our faces and black-face the other side.* . . . That way . . . it looks like we gettin rid of somethin, when we really just addin more to what's already there." (170, my emphasis)

In these images resurgent before and after emancipation, preceding and continuing through the gross stereotyping of the classic minstrel show, Wesley Brown provides an apparently unique Janiform image. There are two special implications here. One is the way actors reinvent an image to face up to trouble without acknowledging awareness that their strategy has a past. Second is the way this black/white face transmits both its backgrounds at once. This image that Brown appears to invent is unlike the usual Janiform representation which typically implies morphing from one to the other—the passing that happens in Michael Jackson's video "Black and White" and in the images Susan Gubar analyzes as "racechanges." The vertically joined face that Brown reiterates is not about merger or passing, not about effacement, not about "gettin rid of somethin." It is about embodying both presences at once: "addin more to what's already there." It is about *compounding* identification. It brings an end to fantasies of passing that leave one or the other behind. It insists on maintaining both together, both visible in the same face.

Brown's novel traffics in plenty of other metamorphosing images. These more familiar poses emphasize an either/or racial dyad. One sees these images as racially this way *or* that, as with the front *or* the back of the character Two-Faced. Alternatively, one sees similarities within conventional opposites, as in black Charmaine's affair with white Sweet Knees Louise. But Brown's image of vertical joining displays the differing features simultaneously taking occupation of the same person. It insists that people who attend, act in, or otherwise obsess about these shows are *both* black *and* white, simultaneously, not escaping from one to the other, not displacing, not subordinating parts of the genealogy. This, then, is the face that rouses riots. Because of this insistent figure, Confederate assassins kill the character Tom Rice and, after the war, vigilantes firebomb the Featherstone show. In the historical heartland Brown contemplates, characters tolerate frequent images of merging. But retrograde citizens will not permit the radically challenging images of forthright compounding.

Outside the novel, this both-at-once imagery is rarer than figures of passing. But it is there and it is stubborn. It appears sometimes in popular culture, as in the vertical black-and-white masks of the Africans who start the dance segment of Michael Jackson's video "Black and White." And it appears periodically in visual art of the black diaspora. Richard Bruce Nugent's "Drawings for Mulattoes" (1927)—by which he must have meant challenges to mulattoes—sketches several variants of these joinings; Stivenson Magloire's Haitian Voudou canvas "Divided Spirit" (1989) renders it memorably. Robert Colescott's *Knowledge of the Past Is the Key to the Future (St. Sebastian)* (1986) is the fullest working of both-at-once compounding. Colescott's title, too, comes very close to Brown's creed.[3] But the root of all these vernacular and vanguard images in the twentieth century is an 1844 minstrel image uncannily like Colescott's. What's more, it is the spitting image of the biracial figure Brown insists on in *Darktown Strutters*.

Although it is extremely unlikely that either Colescott or Brown knew it was there, had certain knowledge that the past was the key to their future, an inaugural instance of the black-and-white vertically joined icon in the western Atlantic was in the very spot that Brown imagined for it. A "divided spirit" had in fact appeared in a now-unknown but entirely actual play by the real T. D. Rice. The play is his important New York street-talk version of the ancient Othello story, staged in Philadelphia, New York, Boston, and Cincinnati during the mid-1840s as *Otello*. Later, in New York, Rice's *Otello* shared the same bill at the National Theatre with the city's first production of *Uncle Tom's Cabin*. In Rice's variant of this tale, Otello and Desdemona have a baby. Desdemona surprises her husband with the child when she comes on stage from the storm in Cypress. Holding the boy up to Otello, she says, "Behold this pledge, your image here is seen." When Otello demurs, she pivots to bring the other side of the child into view, saying, "not this side, love, the other side I mean."[4]

This problem child does not appear in the folk sources that Shakespeare himself drew on, or in Shakespeare's play. Young Otello does not reappear in subsequent Othello variations. After Rice's remarkable image, this baby was aborted until modern visual artists drew it out again in a different vein—and until Brown reproduced it as an imaginative event. The novel's character Jubilee describes the joined image as the focus of "a show that's worth doin." He is right. The joined image is an objective correlative for the profound underlying issues of transracial desire and mimesis that have always been the subtext of the *Othello* story, ever since the Italian folk sources that Shakespeare adapted. Rice's very real play was never published and the prompt script lay purloined in the archives, catalogued under the copyist's name.[5] Yet Brown carries this correlative to us twice in *Darktown Strutters*. How did Wesley Brown figure out this image?

Brown's meditation on the spirit of blackface performance as a troublesome form attempting to smudge the arbitraries of American race led him to seek a vehicle to represent the mutualities of inheritance. He required an image to embody the radical spirit of blackface, which draws performers of all hues to its scabrous pain. Likewise, he needed that image to be in the work of the man known historically as "Daddy" Rice, the old man of blackface. Brown had no way of knowing it was already there. Thus he re-created the truth that the real Tom Rice's career had led him likewise to invent almost a century and a half earlier. Wesley Brown, to his great credit, re-invented a missing link that had in fact existed but was no longer known.

Like Rice before him, Brown enacts what it is to be inescapably afloat in a popular culture, where the currents come in cycles. Their most alluring, most generative modes float again and again on a tide that identifies across race even while other zones of the same culture continually hold those categories distinct and make their crossings taboo. These bodies, the offspring of parents in love, in which the parts stay insistently intact rather than subordinating one another, remain challenging traces of the jarring cultural encounters that industrial dislocations amped up around the world. Blackface performance registered those overlappings early. Popular culture proliferates them. Literature feeds on these spawnings.

Like a good deal of recent fiction, from Don DeLillo to Ishmael Reed, *Darktown Strutters* is unabashedly about both the stereotypes that we, who live media-saturated existences, must inhabit, and the manipulation of these same stereotypes. After exciting these intolerable images and suffering many of their consequences, Jim Crow strays into the novel's ultimate scene, set at the end of Reconstruction: a celebration of the Republic's first Centennial. The scene takes place in East St. Louis—home of Stagolee, Miles Davis, and Chuck Berry—a crossroads at the center of the country where much black performance has cross-pollinated. A mass arrest follows the festivity, a P. T. Barnum "extravaganza" that staged American ethnicities as if they were real —"not a stage show, but the Southland as it really is." Jim Crow walks past "black women and men who wore tags saying what kind of Negro they were . . . The Contented Slave! The Wretched Freedman! The Comic Negro! The Negro Brute! The Tragic Mulatto! The Local Color Negro! and The Exotic Primitive!" (216). As part of this process—not at all dissimilar from the way we all still parade our labels and identities printed, sewn in, and otherwise marked on every purchased costume, even tattooed on our bodies, pasted on our car bumpers—a photographer is capturing images, regardless of the actors' reluctance to participate. "One way or the other your picture's gonna end up in the 'Rogue's Gallery,'" the photographer announces: "It's up to you what kind of shape you want to be in when your picture's taken" (218–219).

How to deal with this mediated economy of stereotypes not one whit limited to Barnum's stockade is likely the most important lesson that *Darktown Strutters* enacts with its own style, images, and imagination. It is no accident that Brown has chosen to investigate and inhabit a role that social forces have pickled, digested, and passed on. The surprising life that he finds still active in this processing does not conclude even in this surreal dead end. Just at the moment that the photographer snaps Jim Crow's picture, "a piece of a dance step that Jim had never thought of before exploded like flash powder in his mind" (219), causing him to jiggle. You cannot say Barnum's photographer caught Jim Crow. Certainly the flash did not freeze him in the intended role: "The Conniving Uncle Tom." However, neither can you say that Jim Crow escaped mediation or surveillance.

What we must say is that Jim Crow is still on the move. While he still struts, the verdict on his meaning and role is inconclusive. He continues to subvert the attempts of his controllers to tie up his package. Jim Crow is just like us, only more so. We continue to have Jim Crow, and other tricksters in his mode, who trouble us by complicating who's who.

1. On 18 October 1830, the *Louisville Public Advertiser* ran an ad asking "Ladies and Gentlemen of the profession, desirous of connecting themselves to a new Circuit of Theatres in contemplation" to contact "Thos. Rice, Manager, Louisville." neither circuit nor company materialized beyond contemplation, and Tom Rice soon joined, oddly enough, J. P. Brown's Theatre and Circus, which played Louisville in mid-November 1830.

2. Alexis de Tocqueville, *Democracy in America,* ed. J. P. Mayer (reprint, 1835, France; 1838, United States) (New York: Harper Perennial, 1988), 489.

3. Charles S. Johnson's *Ebony and Topaz* (1927) first published Nugent's images, which Susan Gubar reprinted in *Racechanges: White Skin, Black Face in American Culture* (New York: Oxford University Press, 1997). Magloire's "Divided Spirit" is reproduced in Karen McCarthy Brown, *Tracing the Spirit: Ethnographic Essays on Haitian Art* (Davenport, Iowa: Davenport Museum of Art; distributed by University of Washington Press, 1995), 67. Colescott's *Knowledge of the Past Is the Key to the Future (St. Sebastian)* is reproduced in Susan Gubar's *Racechanges,* facing page 137.

4. W. T. Lhamon Jr., *Jump Jim Crow: Plays Lyrics, and Street Prose of the First Atlantic Popular Culture* (Cambridge: Harvard University Press, forthcom-

ing 2001). I have found playbills naming the child actors who fleshed out "Young Otello" on stage, embodying this both-at-once icon.

5. The manuscript of *Otello,* which I edited for publication in *Jump Jim Crow,* is in the Billy Rose Theatre Collection of the New York Public Library, filed under "John Wright." Stage manager of the Tremont Theatre in Boston in the mid-nineteenth century, Wright wrote on the first page of his *Otello* prompt script, "Copied by permission of His friend T. D. Rice, Esq."

FURTHER READING

Brown, Wesley. *Tragic Magic.* New York: Random House, 1978.

Ellison, Ralph. "An Extravagance of Laughter." In *The Collected Essays of Ralph Ellison*, edited by John H. Callahan. New York: Modern Library, 1995.

Gubar, Susan. *Racechanges: White Skin, Black Face in American Culture.* New York: Oxford University Press, 1997.

Lhamon, W. T., Jr. *Jump Jim Crow: Plays Lyrics, and Street Prose of the First Atlantic Popular Culture.* Cambridge: Harvard University Press, forthcoming 2001.

———. *Raising Cain: Blackface Performance from Jim Crow to Hip Hop.* Cambridge: Harvard University Press, 1998.

Sollors, Werner. *Neither White nor Black, Yet Both: Thematic Explorations of Interracial Literature.* 1997. Reprint, Cambridge: Harvard University Press, 1999.

Toll, Robert. *Blacking Up: The Minstrel Show in Nineteenth-Century America.* New York: Oxford University Press, 1974.